TRINITY AND THE HEISTERS

Trevor Holliday

Barnstork Press

ISBN-13: 9798454185459
ISBN-10: 1477123456

Cover design by: John M. Holliday
Library of Congress Control Number: 2018675309
Printed in the United States of America

To El Charro Café
Serving fine food in
Tucson, Arizona for 100 years.

CONTENTS

WET AND WILD

Frank Trinity needed the haircut. He could have done without the game show.

"Same as always, right?"

Joe Dominguez kept the barber shop on Sixth Street. He was putting a new blade into his safety razor.

Joe wasn't watching the show himself, but had the volume on high. Trinity heard Bob Eubanks yucking it up with the competing couples.

Joe's barber shop was no-nonsense. The place smelled like Alberto VO5. Next to the mirror, Joe displayed his barber's license and a small framed Niño de Atocha. The Panasonic color television behind Trinity was new. Sitting in the barber chair Trinity saw a mirrored reflection of the program.

"You want your sideburns shorter?" Joe said. "You got one's a little longer than the other. You going Engelbert Humperdinck now?"

He spoke louder than usual to be heard over the television.

"Just even them up," Trinity said. "It's hard for me to see if they're even when I'm shaving.

One of the newlywed men turned red after his

wife answered a question about making whoopee.

Trinity didn't hear what she said, but the audience was laughing.

"That couple? They're not gonna last long like that," Joe said.

Trinity shrugged.

One of the wives was hitting her husband over the head with the cardboard he'd written his answer on.

"You think this show's for real?" Joe said.

"It's got to be real," Trinity said. "They get in trouble otherwise. They can lose their license."

"I dunno," Joe said. "It looks fake in a way. I mean, who's going on there and answering those kinda questions? And for what? The prizes aren't great."

Trinity didn't answer. He was watching the waterbed ad. He'd seen it before.

A beautiful woman on the bed faced the camera.

Candles. Soothing music.

Trinity knew what was coming.

The camera caressed the woman's face. A picture of peaceful serenity.

"Malibu Waterbeds, giving you the restful sleep your body needs at night."

Then drums.

Bam-di-di-bam-bam-bam.

The same woman. Standing now. Blonde hair cascading around her shoulders.

A look of total abandon.

Ann-Margret in *Bye Bye Birdie*.

Her voice low and sensual.

"But we're wet and wild... When you want."

"That's a hell of an ad," Joe said. "Think it sells waterbeds?"

Trinity nodded.

The commercial told its story in less than forty seconds.

Not an easy feat.

"It got *me* thinking," Trinity said.

EL CHARRO

The limbs of the mesquite trees in front of the adobe houses were hung with strings of Italian lights making shadows on the sidewalk.

The Presidio of Tucson looked like a Mexican silver mining village at night.

The moon, although nearly full on the edge of the dark violet sky, was obscured by a dark cloud moving across its face.

Tuesday night in the part of October when you might start wearing a sweater against a possible chill.

Frank Trinity's hat cast a shadow under the muted yellow beam of the streetlight. He looked through a bramble of mesquite branches near the Corner Market on Meyer and Franklin.

He paused for a moment, enjoying the last few minutes of the evening before continuing toward his house.

Trinity had just left El Charro. The conversation with the woman seated at the table next to Trinity had been unexpected but pleasant. They were the only customers in the small side room of the Tucson restaurant.

Just Trinity and the woman seated side by side under the decades-old calendars.

Like two people in an old black and white movie thrown together by chance.

She was beautiful, of course, with dark hair.

Dressed as if she expected to meet someone at El Charro.

Trinity and the woman were seated so closely to each other, it would have been awkward not to at least exchange friendly greetings.

She broke the silence before the waitress, warning them about the hot plates, put their dinners down in front of them.

"This is a pretty quiet night for El Charro, isn't it?" the woman said.

"It is," he said. "Where are the mariachis?"

She laughed.

"Maybe they can convince you to sing?"

"I don't think that's such a good idea," he said.

"It's usually only empty like this on game days," she said.

They both ordered carne seca.

She was having a second margarita. Lifting the drink to her lips, looking at Trinity.

Her dark business suit and ivory white blouse were not out of place in the cool fall evening.

On the middle finger of her right hand she wore a silver thunderbird signet ring. A man's ring. In the center was a piece of intensely blue lapis lazuli.

"Beautiful ring," Trinity said.

She looked at it and turned it on her finger.

"I've had it forever," she said. "I've got some earrings that go with it. I should have worn them."

She asked Trinity if there was anything else to order at El Charro besides the carne seca. He shook his head and said no there was not. The carne seca was the best item on the menu.

They chatted at first about the weather, then about the news. She told Trinity she had lived in Tucson all her life.

"We've always lived here," she said.

"We?" Trinity said.

He didn't say it intentionally. It slipped out. Husband? He looked around.

She laughed.

She meant she and her sister had always lived in Tucson.

It was a *hang-up.*

She laughed again telling this to Trinity. She always said *we*, even though she was three years older than her sister. We, just like Queen Victoria.

"She's been on my mind," she said, "my sister, not Victoria."

Trinity nodded. He said he understood. He knew this was his cue to to ask another question about the sister, but he didn't.

"My sister's name is Grace," she said. "I know you've seen her. Everybody has."

Trinity raised his eyebrows, but said nothing.

He could have asked why the woman's sister was on her mind? This kind of situation was supposed to be his specialty. Drawing information out of women he had barely met. Instead, he looked at the vintage calendar above his table. The date read 1948 and in the painting a vaquero and a beautiful senorita gazed at the sunset.

Trinity didn't ask about the sister.

He could have, but he didn't.

The woman shook her head and smiled. An attractive and well-practiced smile. A sales presentation smile. Attractive enough, perhaps, to make a dull presentation bearable.

She looked at Trinity a moment longer than necessary, but her eyes were steady.

"I'm sorry," Trinity said. "My name's Frank Trinity."

Her name was Lydia Partridge.

He had never seen her in El Charro before. He would have noticed her if he had. He hoped he would see her again.

They exchanged cards. She was in sales, she told him. She shook a cigarette out of a half-empty pack.

"I'm cutting down," she said. "It's really hard to break the habit, though."

Trinity nodded.

"Yes it is," he said. "Maybe the hardest."

She also liked talking with people, she said, and was glad Trinity had been here tonight.

It would have been lonely otherwise.

"My hours are so unpredictable," she said. "I'm never exactly sure where I'll be at any given time."

Trinity also liked talking with people, more or

less. He was certainly happy to talk with Lydia.

She worked at the Malibu Waterbeds on Speedway.

"Is that the one with the blonde woman in the ads?"

Lydia nodded then shook her head.

"You've seen those. I guess everyone has. That's actually my sister, the one I mentioned. She does ads. She's something, isn't she?"

"The two of you look alike. I'm sure you've heard that."

The sister's features were very close to those of Lydia's.

"At least once or twice," she said. "I'm having a margarita, are you?"

Trinity shook his head. Not tonight.

Lydia smiled. Sighed. Put the cigarette in the ashtray. Looked away from Trinity at a place on the wall not even close to his face.

"I don't have to drive. My new place is so close I can walk."

"Beautiful night, tonight," he said. "It's the time of the year."

"Beautiful," she said.

Trinity gave her one of his cards and Lydia looked at it, then put it in her purse.

FRANK TRINITY INVESTIGATIONS
Franklin Street,
Tucson, Arizona.

Usually people said something about the investigations part.

Lydia didn't.

She just looked at the card.

"I love this place," she said. "I'm surprised I haven't seen you here before. Of course, it's usually packed, isn't it?"

Trinity nodded.

She looked at him.

"I like your name," she said. "It really fits you. It's solid."

"Solid?"

She laughed.

Took another drink of the margarita.

"Like the Rock of Gibraltar."

MANZANITA ROOM

Grace Partridge was a blonde in her thirties. She had the look of a fashion model and gave nothing away with the expression on her face.

Tony Franklin was making a drink for Big Bobby Phillips. Bobby had been drinking Crown Royals, but now he wanted a Harvey Wallbanger.

"You won't believe the way this guy makes them," Bobby said. "Watch him, Grace. He's the maestro."

Grace knew Tony better than Bobby. She was talking things over with Bobby at the Manzanita Room at the Western Way. Listening to Big Bobby give last minute instructions.

In the full length plate glass window, the nearly full moon cast light over the saguaros.

"You're confident," Big Bobby said. "I like that. I like that a lot. I mean, who the hell doesn't like that? You look confident, and that's important. You don't have confidence, what have you got?"

Big Bobby had the fast patter of a motivational speaker. Fast patter and a good tan.

"Easy on the Galliano, right Tony?"

Tony held up the tall bottle with the yellow liqueur.

"I can skip it entirely, you want, Bobby."

"No, no, no." Big Bobby shook his shoulder-length gray hair. "Gotta hide some in there, who's kidding who?"

Bobby turned to Grace.

"You're gonna love this, honest. Take just an eensy-weensy taste you won't believe the way he does it. He makes 'em great."

Grace looked at Tony.

Raised her eyebrows. *Can-you-believe-this-guy?*

Bobby kept on talking.

"Any last minute things we got to go over? Anything at all. Now's the time. Speak now, or forever hold your peace. Baby, you know I heard that *last* bit enough over the years."

Bobby laughed at his own joke.

Grace looked at him.

"That and the until death do us part. Never again, though. Seriously, I've given you what you need for this guy. The guy with the you-know-whats."

Bobby lifted his hands, holding his fingers out like pistols.

"Don't forget, baby, he's kinda short in stature. Diminutive. Don't say anything about him being short, though. He's sensitive."

Tony Franklin could have heard them a little better if he wanted to snoop.

He ignored the part about Grace going to see a guy about guns. Some things, you don't need to know about.

The Western Way Resort was going for authenticity with the new decor. First they'd taken out the old mauve rugs. Now there were enormous earth-toned paintings on the walls and the restrooms smelled like sandalwood.

Native American flute piped into the Manzanita Room on a continuous loop.

Tony liked the music fine at first, but after about an hour it had started to get on his nerves.

Grace, who had done some acting, lowered her eyes while looking up at Bobby.

Tony, standing behind Big Bobby, noticed Grace's expression. He turned away toward the row of bottles behind the bar so Bobby wouldn't see his grin.

Tony was making Grace the drink she liked, grapefruit juice and vodka over the rocks.

Big Bobby was being a control freak with the Harvey Wallbanger thing. Trying to get Grace to try it. Like this was some pickup bar at the airport.

Tony turned back.

"You okay there, boss?" Tony said.

Big Bobby was leaning over from the barstool, rubbing his right knee. Still talking, despite the uncomfortable position.

Bobby had been talking about Telluride, Vail, and Aspen with Tony before Grace came in.

Ski talk.

Big Bobby would be wasting time if he stayed here this winter with the powder they would be getting in Colorado.

Not everyone knows how to ski in powder, right?

According to Big Bobby, Colorado wasn't the same scene like you had there a few years ago. The place was all money and the glitz nowadays.

Not like when he'd first arrived there, but what did Bobby know back then? He was just a ski-bum with jeans and a pair of Heads.

He shoulda bought real estate, that's what he shoulda done before the boom. Things weren't the same there anymore now, all commercial. Nothing ever was the same, was it?

Bobby always wore shorts and sandals. Even on the slopes, man.

He was a well-tanned five foot eight.

Today he wore a purple and white striped surfer shirt with an iron cross pendant nestled in gray chest hair.

White sunglasses.

Gotta hand it to Big Bobby. He had cultivated a look and he stayed with it.

The Harvey Wallbanger was in front of Bobby, practically untouched.

"Look," he said. "I can't drink that. Too much sugar. I just can't."

He looked at Grace.

"You want it? You got that fruit juice crap going anyway."

Grace shook her head no.

"You want something else?" Tony said.

"Yeah sure," Bobby said.

He pointed at his tumbler, now empty. He'd already applied the ice from the glass to his knee. "Shit, you don't have to ask, do you? Hit me with the Crown again. My frigging knee's killing me. "

"You got it," Tony said.

"Wages of sin, right?" Big Bobby said. "What I need is a Darvon."

Grace leaned toward Bobby.

Put her hand on his knee and rubbed.

"Everything's fine, Bobby. They drop the car off to me, I pick you up. It's easy." She nodded toward Tony. "He didn't hear anything, if that's got you worried."

Bobby shook his head. Pushed Grace's hand away and resumed his own rubbing.

"Nothing's got me worried, baby," he said. "What gave you that idea?"

"I don't know, Bobby," she said. "We've gone over this, haven't we? I mean, it's not complicated. You put it all together. It's gonna be fine. Trust me."

Bobby downed the Crown Royal and dropped from the barstool.

"Gotta see a man about a horse," he said.

Winked at Tony.

"Catch you later."

Tony Franklin watched Big Bobby head toward the men's room.

Bobby had a paunch. Hiding it was difficult

with the knee, but Bobby gave it a try with both shoulders thrown back.

Tony turned to Grace.

"You driving him home?

Grace sipped the grapefruit vodka.

Put it down.

Dipped her finger to stir.

She nodded.

"I'm full service, Tony. You know that."

CLOSING TIME

Lydia Partridge didn't want to go home, but she couldn't stay here. The last thing she wanted was to have a problem here at the restaurant. She liked the place and she wanted to keep coming here. She looked at the business card.

Frank Trinity Investigations.

Franklin Street was close to the restaurant. It wouldn't take a minute. She could walk directly there. Knock on the door. It would be romantic.

Strangers in the Night.

Why not? His place was just around the corner. It would be simple to walk there, even in her heels.

His place would be like a Bogart movie. He had had plenty of time to get home, hadn't he?

Lydia had noticed his scuffed cowboy boots. He would have them up on his desk, just like Sam Spade.

Maybe he would have a bottle of rye in the drawer.

Make yourself comfortable, sweetheart.

She would stand at his door waiting. There would be a look of surprise, but not disappointment on his face.

He would be far from disappointed, seeing her standing at his doorstep.

She made the first move by giving him her card. She was certain she had given her card first.

The waitress was nowhere to be seen. The busboy was sweeping the room. The door to the kitchen was open and she heard the dishwasher running.

Meatloaf was singing on the radio.

Two Out of Three Ain't Bad.

I want you. I need you.

They were trying to close.

She would spare herself the embarrassment of ordering another margarita.

Lydia looked at the card again. She would get up.

Pay her bill.

Walk to his house.

But she knew this wasn't an old movie.

He wasn't Humphrey Bogart.

Sam Spade didn't wear cowboy boots.

She pictured him at the door, looking down at her.

A concerned expression on his face would turn to desire.

She would tell him about her sister. What she knew about her so far. What she dreaded finding out.

He was an investigator, so she would have to pay him for his services. They wouldn't necessarily have to get personally involved. Although they might.

There was still the last sip of the margarita. She tipped the glass to her lips. It was closing time here, but there were other places.

This wasn't the only game in this town.

She looked at his card again. Was this the right time?

Frank Trinity. She shook her head.

This wasn't the right time. She wouldn't ask him for help tonight.

THE SECRET GARDEN

Grace Partridge stood on the cracked sidewalk in front of Lydia's house. The moon illuminated a patch of the adobe wall.

What a difference a little drive made.

She had driven from the foothills.

From the Manzanita Room at the Western Way to *this* neighborhood.

A twenty minute drive.

Lydia insisted on calling the place a *barrio*. Which was just another one of her sister's affectations. The neighborhood was an overpriced dump.

It was depressing, but Grace still came to her sister's house often. Not as often now as she had previously. Sometimes, when she had needed the money, she took cash Lydia had left for her.

Things were different now.

She hadn't needed money from Lydia for a while.

She looked down the street. There was no more sign of life here than there ever was.

The streetlights were barely bright enough to

lighten the deeply recessed entryway.

Lydia had paid a bundle for the row house, but the place still looked shabby.

Why Lydia lived in this part of town was beyond Grace.

Grace couldn't imagine living like Lydia.

Grace's own apartment complex was filled with energy. Nonstop parties every day of the week.

Living there was *fun*.

Lydia's place was a morgue. You might as well be dead if you lived here.

Lydia didn't know what she was missing.

Grace stopped at the door.

Listened.

Lydia wasn't home yet.

That was good.

Lydia had let Grace have a key, and sometimes Grace felt like slumming.

She let herself in but stopped herself from turning on the lights.

Casa Lydia.

Grace didn't like being in the dark. The adobe walls felt claustrophobic.

Grace could barely look at the icons Lydia displayed on the walls.

Old wooden saints in agony.

Sebastian, filled with arrows.

Grace knew what she was looking for. Lydia wouldn't be back until later. Maybe Lydia was on one of her own midnight prowls she thought were secret.

Grace shook her head.

It didn't matter what Lydia was doing. Grace didn't care what Lydia was doing or with whom she was doing it. She walked down the narrow hallway to Lydia's bedroom, carefully turning her eyes while walking past the old saints in their silver frames.

Even in the dark, the icons stared at Grace.

Lydia's bedroom, of course, was neat. Lydia never left her bed unmade.

Grace turned on a lamp and pulled open the drawer of the bedside table.

The nickel-plated automatic lay in the drawer.

Grace checked to make sure the clip was full.

The automatic was her sister's version of home defense. Probably effective, though Grace couldn't imagine Lydia shooting anyone.

Next to the automatic was a copy of *The Secret Garden*. Grace picked up the antique book from the drawer. She held the worn green cover in her hands. How typical of Lydia to keep this book by the side of her bed.

The Secret Garden.

Lydia's favorite book.

Grace shook her head. She remembered trying to read it years ago at Lydia's insistence.

The story bored her. Whiny brats in a musty old house with a garden.

The garden's a secret, don't tell anybody.

Please.

Grace preferred Mickey Spillane, the ones with

the lurid covers like their father read.

Killer Mine.

Now *that* was a book.

Under the book, of course, Lydia kept her cash. Grace left the money undisturbed.

Grace stood up.

Kept the lamp on and walked to the bathroom.

Looked at herself in the mirror then opened the medicine cabinet.

She needed to leave before Lydia returned, but couldn't resist staying longer. Coming here felt like habit.

Lydia liked analyzing Grace. She said Grace was obsessive.

Lydia didn't know the half of it. Grace's life was completely different from Lydia's.

She went back to Lydia's bed and sat down again. She slid the drawer out and lifted out the automatic.

The word *RAVEN* was etched on the side of the gun.

This wasn't exactly what she needed. The Raven was strictly a backup weapon. With such a low caliber the gun was probably not very useful except at extremely short range.

But it wouldn't hurt to have it with her, would it?

She had enough money for the real weaponry.

Bobby, she couldn't bring herself to call him Big Bobby, had given her the guy's name and the cash.

Don't say anything about his height. He's sensitive.

That was what Big Bobby said.

Big Bobby.

What a laugh.

Grace stopped.

There was somebody else in the house.

She turned the lamp off and looked at the bedroom door. Grace was familiar with all the creaks and groans the place made, and she was familiar with the tread of Lydia's feet.

This wasn't Lydia.

Too heavy.

Much too heavy.

The handle of the pistol felt warm in her hands.

Even in the dark Grace could see the outlines of the room.

She pointed the Raven at the center of the bedroom door.

GIBRALTAR

Trinity thought about Lydia Partridge's comment while walking home.

Lydia still drinking margaritas after Trinity left. He had stood up first.

She was finishing her third margarita and had ordered a fourth.

Funny she mentioned Gibraltar. Trinity had been to Gibraltar.

He'd gone to a NATO training there with British counterparts, flying into the tiny airport, the pilot negotiating the narrow foggy strip surrounded by the sea from the cockpit of a specially adapted de Havilland Comet.

Trinity remembered the flight attendant.

Breezy and cordial at takeoff, by the end of the flight he saw her gripping her tea trolley and looking bilious.

The small hotel had starched sheets and a view of the rock.

Trinity's British counterparts were fun-loving.

They wanted to talk about the states. They wanted to talk about *Dallas* and whoever had shot J.R. Ewing.

The one British woman looked like Emma Peel.

Her name was Pamela Roscoe.

During a free afternoon, Trinity and Pamela had taken the cable car, gone through the siege tunnels and enjoyed the sunshine.

They overheard a guide wearing a Union Jack bowler describing the Pillars of Hercules. The rock itself had been more impressive than Trinity expected.

After training that evening, Trinity and Pamela went to a place featuring a Dutch band called *Star Spangled Watermelon*. Predictably, the band played Lynyrd Skynyrd. Trinity remembered the dual lead guitars and a twenty minute version of *Tuesday's Gone*. He had played darts, but not too much.

There had been monkeys on the northern side of the rock. Pamela Roscoe used the word 'beastly' to describe them.

"*Beastly* things, aren't they?"

That was what Trinity knew about Gibraltar.

Lydia's card was in his pocket.

LYDIA PARTRIDGE
MALIBU WATERBEDS
SPEEDWAY BOULEVARD

Lydia was possibly thirty years old.

She had dark hair and displayed a sense of humor along with intelligence.

Trinity should have liked her. He could have

stayed at El Charro and they could have talked about the vintage calendars and what was new in the world of waterbeds, but Trinity decided to leave.

He wondered what she meant by the Gibraltar comment?

It was a meaningless non-sequitur. Odd.

Trinity found the remark troubling.

Lydia had been worried. She hadn't looked at him in his eyes, instead she focused on the side of Trinity's face. Turning away. Telling him a lie.

Only a slight give-away movement in her hands. Just this side of a tremble. Something on her mind. More than her sister.

Trinity turned the light on in the front room. The pierced tin lamp barely lighted the room. Sitting on the leather chair, Trinity took Lydia's card from his shirt pocket.

Malibu Waterbeds. Speedway.

He thought about the commercials. The sister was a blonde version of Lydia.

Lydia and Grace Partridge.

The commercials were splashy, loud, and persistent.

It was late.

Trinity looked at Lydia's card again. Placed it next to the telephone. He pulled his boots off and leaned back in the chair. The brim of his hat dropped over his eyes.

THE TOP OF CAMPBELL

Lydia parked her Datsun 280Z on the street in front of Trinity's house. She set the emergency brake and looked toward the window in front.

Under a light in the window she saw his profile.

She smoked a cigarette in the darkness then put it out in the car's ashtray.

Watched the window. Trying to make a decision.

Released the emergency brake. Started the car.

It was early to go home. She couldn't face going home, but she couldn't knock on his door.

Twenty minutes took Lydia to the top of Campbell.

She got out of the car and looked at the lights of the city.

The diamond necklace. Lights shimmering east to west.

Why hadn't she knocked on his door?

It would have been easy.

She could have just knocked on his door.

Trinity would have taken care of the rest.

URBAN COWBOY

When he went out to party, Calvin Gamble always dressed western. At the Crazy Horse, Calvin wore jeans, cowboy shirt. The threads were fly as shit. The cowboy hat, the one with the feathered band like Richard Petty wore, he'd taken from a house in Flowing Wells.

Party clothes like Richard Roundtree would wear going to Gilley's in Pasadena, Texas.

He never wore these clothes on the job.

Calvin needed to keep a nondescript look when he was working. Depending on weather, he'd put on some jeans and a T-shirt. Sneakers and maybe a wind-breaker. Something you wouldn't notice or wouldn't remember if you saw him.

He was too tall for a break-in man. So he'd been told. You need to be agile and wiry. In this field, small was better.

Calvin Gamble wasn't small.

But Calvin Gamble was also smart, and a quick study.

Calvin had never met a home-security system he couldn't beat given enough time and enough motivation. He knew successful burglary required more than the ability to get into a house. A successful break-in man had to be able to get *out* of a house, too, no matter what the situation. Burglary wasn't as easy as some people thought. There were plenty of dudes in prison who weren't cut out for the business in the first place. Steal some piece of shit, then try to sell it.

Junkies, mostly.

They gave hard-working professionals like Calvin a bad name.

Calvin was different. Calvin had finesse combined with instincts. He had never come close to getting caught doing a job and he didn't intend to allow such a thing to ever happen.

And Calvin Gamble didn't plan to be a break-in man forever. He knew his skills would take him farther.

He just needed to be on the lookout for opportunity.

Calvin Gamble liked the Crazy Horse.

He liked watching the girls try out the mechanical bull. He never rode the bull himself, but it was fun to watch.

Calvin was not drinking much tonight, just a weaker than usual gin and tonic.

The bouncer had stamped his hand and told Calvin not to be an asshole tonight.

Maybe the dude had mistaken Calvin for somebody else, but on account of the bouncer's size, Calvin didn't challenge him. The dude was a giant.

Calvin was just killing time, really.

He was thinking about changing his name to Bud, like John Travolta in Urban Cowboy.

Bud would be about ten times a better name than Calvin ever had been.

Calvin watched wannabe cowboys take turns on the bull. He scoped women coming into the bar in tight little giggling clusters.

One per group usually worth a second look.

Calvin looked at his watch. The light up dial told him it was time to get moving.

There was nothing for him here tonight.

One of women in the back looked like the other actress in Urban Cowboy. The one who *wasn't* Debra Winger. Tall, dark haired, perfectly fitting Jordache jeans.

If Calvin hadn't decided he was doing a job tonight, and if the woman hadn't been talking to a big, angry looking man, Calvin might have gone up, adjusted his jeans, and talked to her.

He might have asked her if she wanted a drink.

No reason not to.

Hell, the drinks were cheap here.

Why not.

Just walk right up like John Travolta would.

Hey, my name's Bud.

The bouncer gave Calvin a look when he left.

Shook his head like he was laughing.

It only took Calvin a few minutes to get downtown from West Lester Street.

The front seat of the Country Squire warmed up

quick. One thing you had to give Ford was their air conditioning and their heaters. Calvin was no fan of either a hot or a cold car.

He discovered the neighborhood when he'd made a wrong turn downtown, coming out of a place called the Daylighter Bar.

The Daylighter had been fine, but it had a corporate clientele, and Calvin felt at a disadvantage there.

Most of the clientele were in some kind of profession, and although Calvin was a good burglar, he didn't feel this was going to win him points at the Daylighter. He left before there was a scene. Sometimes things got out of control at bars, but the fault never lay with Calvin.

After he saw the pocket neighborhood, he'd scouted it on foot a couple of times.

He bought a churro from a sidewalk vendor and watched the comings and goings in the area from a park bench. The cars were the give-away. There might as well have been neon dollar signs flashing on the street signs.

The neighborhood was old, but not shabby. This was one of those places rich white people loved.

The people in this downtown neighborhood wouldn't be gun-owners, either.

The signs in their windows and yards made that clear.

Give peace a chance.

Fine with Calvin Gamble who didn't like the idea of a stepping in front of the business end of a firearm on one of his midnight rambles.

There were law offices, architectural firms, art galleries in the area, but Calvin Gamble wasn't interested in any of those. He had his eye on a row of adobes, specifically the one on the end. The place looked simple to enter. The woman who lived here, lived here alone, and she had money.

Calvin would go in through the front door, then leave through the back alley.

He didn't want anything bigger than his backpack. He could always ditch the bag, if needed.

Jewelry or cash. Shiny, valuable shit, or money. You could fit a lot into a backpack.

Getting into the house took Calvin less than a minute. He used a bump key, but could have used a nail file for all the resistance the lock gave. He ignored the octagonal security sign. If he heard something, he'd be out in a flash.

The lights were off. The woman who lived there was out.

A sharp-looking dark haired woman.

Calvin knew her habits.

She wouldn't be home for hours.

* * *

The woman in the bedroom surprised Calvin.

She wasn't dark-haired. She was blonde, and she was pointing a tiny automatic at Calvin's chest.

Some kind of pearl handled peashooter.

Probably saw him coming in the bedroom

doorway with his backpack and flashlight.

She was in the dark, rummaging around in a bedside drawer.

Calvin had startled her while she was going through her sister's things.

"You're a friend of Lydia?"

Just like that. Cool as could be.

You're a friend of Lydia?

Like Lydia's friends broke in all the time.

Mi casa es su casa, amigo, right?

Calvin put his hands up. Both of them.

Surrendering.

"I think I'm in the wrong house."

He backed toward the door.

The line of adobe houses looked alike from the outside.

The woman didn't believe him, but she didn't look alarmed, either.

"You're lying, aren't you?" she said.

She stood up and walked toward him, training the gun on Calvin.

Her pose straight from *Charlie's Angels*.

"What are you doing in here?" she said.

Calvin surprised himself by telling her the truth.

"I broke in, but I'm leaving. Put the gun down and I'll go."

There was a look on her face.

She didn't shoot Calvin.

She lowered the gun slowly and pointed toward the bed. Motioning toward him. Patting the bed next to where she sat.

Calvin's hands still above his head.

The flashlight made patterns on the ceiling over the bed.

"I'm leaving," he said. "I'm walking straight out the door."

"Not yet," she said. "I need to talk to you."

VERY
SUPERSTITIOUS

Calvin wasn't interested in the woman's offer.

Some things were just too good to be true. This sounded like one of them.

"Relax," she said. "Listen."

She sat close to Calvin, right next to him on the double bed, carefully looking in his eyes.

He kept his eyes on her, but his hands were also still in the air.

"My name is Grace," she said.

Grace put the gun away, slipping it into her purse like used tissue.

She wasn't going to shoot him.

She could have shot him, she could have screamed, she could have run from the room into the cool, dark, night.

She didn't do any of those things.

Instead, Grace asked Calvin Gamble if he wanted to rob a bank.

Well, she didn't ask him directly. First, she looked at him. Nice eyes she had, but maybe a little crazy.

"You look tough," she said. "I like that."

If they had been standing next to each other next to the mechanical bull at the Outlaw, or at the bar at Carlos Murphy's, something like that, Calvin would have played along, acting charmed. But this wasn't happy hour and Calvin was sitting on a bed with a woman who up until a few seconds before had held a firearm close enough to do some real damage to his chest even though the thing was probably low caliber and not particularly accurate.

Calvin scowled.

"Yeah, exactly," she said, nodding. "Your eyes when you do that. You're tough, but smart. Am I right?"

"Kinda," Calvin said.

He figured he was tough as anyone else.

Smarter, for sure.

She told him about the project.

That's what she called the robbery. It was a *project*.

She looked at Calvin. Said he would be perfect.

"It's way up on Oracle," she said, as if the specific location made no difference. "It's not even *around* here. It's an amazing plan. I think I just needed to find *you*."

She looked at him.

Despite his better judgment, Calvin kept looking at her.

Robbing a bank.

She wanted him to go from Double-A straight to

the major leagues.

"Do you think everything happens for a reason?" she said. "I do."

Calvin knew a smarter person would find a way to get up and walk away from the bed.

Get the hell out of there.

Instead, Calvin stayed.

Maybe he stayed because of her good looks or maybe on account of the way she was looking at him. There were only inches separating them on the undisturbed double bed.

"Something like that," Calvin said, "a plan like that, if you don't get yourself killed, you wind up in Florence. Not me, not a chance."

Grace looked at him. A fleck of yellow in her right eye. Probably why it looked crazy. But the eye was also interesting.

Calvin watched Grace and watched her eye.

"What's your name," she said. "Tell me the truth."

"Calvin," he said.

He was getting a strange feeling. He felt a combination of dread and fascination looking at her. He remembered watching a hypnotist on Merv Griffin. The hypnotist told Merv how a person couldn't be hypnotized without their own participation. Calvin recalled this, but the memory was getting hazy.

"My friends call me Bud," he said.

Calvin heard himself saying the words, almost as if another person was talking.

Grace was speaking slowly, softly. Explaining something to him. Going through the plan in a very gentle, relaxing way.

"I don't know, Bud," she said. "This is something very special for you to consider. It's an opportunity. It literally fell in my lap. And it's falling into your lap now."

"Robbing a bank? That's something fell in your lap?"

"The man I know is an expert."

"And you're the driver?"

Grace nodded. Solemnly.

Calvin looked at her again.

Grace was serious.

"I'm the driver. You should see me drive. You're going to be impressed. Bobby's got a thing about it. He's very superstitious. Bobby has to have a woman driver or he just won't do it. "

"Where do I come into this?"

He had to ask. He knew it was a bad idea, but he had to ask.

Grace scooched closer to him on the bed. Their faces were inches apart in the nearly dark room.

"He has a good plan," Grace said. "He knows exactly what he's doing."

"I don't know," Calvin said.

"You should relax," Grace said. "Relax. You're too tense."

She moved closer to him, touched his shoulders and brought him forward.

She kissed him.

A dry kiss, but there was some feeling behind it. Calvin had an odd sensation.

He wondered if this was what it felt like to have your life pass before your eyes.

SNOW AND NEALLEY

Value Village filled a block on Fourth Avenue.

Trinity went into the thrift store looking for books. After finding two Simenons and an Ed McBain, Trinity did a quick turnaround to see what else had come in since his last visit.

On the iron blade of an axe, Trinity found etched the name of the maker:

Snow and Nealley
Manufactured in Smyrna, Maine.

A good manufacturer. Trinity remembered reading about them. This particular axe had to be at least eighty years old. Hard to figure how it got from the woods of Maine to the desert in Tucson. No question about buying it. The axe would be around for years after Trinity owned it. Trinity held the axe in both hands like the statue of Paul Bunyan on Grant Road.

He could sharpen the Snow and Nealley, but it was already in pretty good shape.

The hickory shaft was fine. He could oil it, but

the axe felt balanced and ready.

Thirteen dollars and fifty cents. Twelve for the axe and a buck and a half for the books.

The woman at the register looked at the axe and then at the books.

"That's it?" she said.

Trinity smiled.

"This is plenty," he said. "Winter's coming."

The Tucson sun greeted Trinity when he walked out of Value Village.

High noon for Big Paul.

He held the axe by his side. Walked toward Sixth Street to the the Bronco.

Thinking about Lydia, the woman last night at El Charro.

She had given Trinity her card.

Maybe she needed his help.

Then again, maybe she just wanted Trinity to have her phone number.

Either way, it wouldn't hurt to call her.

MI CASITA

Calvin Gamble, wearing a short sleeved cotton cowboy shirt and bootcut blue jeans, sat in the driver's seat of his Country Squire station wagon in the parking lot outside the Mi Casita Motel on Tucson's Miracle Mile.

Parking next to the pool so he could watch the place.

For this kind of work he didn't need to blend into the background. He could dress up a little.

It was Wednesday, almost noon. Grace had given him money and a card with the room number where he would meet the man.

Calvin smoked a Kool cigarette, blowing one smoke ring after another through the station wagon's driver side vent window.

If he had second thoughts about moving up from his life of breaking and entering to a new career in bank robbery, he showed no sign.

Cool and confident. Sitting in the car while the sun blazed outside in the middle of the day.

Eddie Rabbitt on the radio.

Calvin turned it up.

Driving My Life Away.

Looking in the rear view mirror, Calvin Gamble got a good look at himself.

Liked what he saw.

He glanced at the Timex.

He had bought it for the silver and turquoise band at the Tanque Verde Swap Meet. The watch might be turning out to be some kind of good luck thingy.

Just like if Calvin had leaned over a pool table and sent all the stripes out teetering next to all six pockets on the break.

All but one, which dropped.

All Calvin had to do now was tap the rest of the balls in.

He took his eyes off the watch and took another drag on the Kool.

Hating to wait.

Calvin looked at his watch again. The big hand needed to reach twelve.

Time was standing still. Grace told him specifically to wait for the man.

Do *not* go to his room early.

Calvin looked at the watch again, at the red stones next to the turquoise.

The watch *had* brought him luck.

Grace could have shot him. The most he could have reasonably hoped for was to get out of the row house alive.

Instead, he was watching his life change right in front of his damn eyes.

Grace told Calvin Gamble about Bobby Phillips.

Big Bobby.

That's what the others called him. Grace told Calvin he could just called him Bobby if he wanted.

Calvin was bigger than Bobby, so it wouldn't make sense for Calvin to call him Big Bobby.

Calvin wanted to be agreeable so either way was fine.

Grace had met Bobby Phillips up at the Western Way. She was friends with the bartender there.

Bobby Phillips wanted pretty women to drive him on his jobs? Grace was as pretty as they came.

Grace looked like that French actress. The one on the Vespa. The actress had posed for Life Magazine wearing dark glasses and smoking a cigarette. That picture made an impression on Calvin.

Calvin also figured out Grace was the sexy blonde in those waterbed commercials. Grace hadn't said anything about them, but Calvin recognized her.

She was kind of a celebrity.

Big Bobby was planning the bank job up in Casas Adobes, a snitzy location on the north side of town.

By now, Calvin and Grace were just calling it *the job.*

Grace told Calvin she had talked Big Bobby into using Calvin as second gunman.

Second gunman, she said.

Like they were casting a school play.

She said she'd made Calvin sound like the second coming of Harry Pierpont.

Grace knew a lot about bank robbers.

"Dillinger's right-hand-man was Harry Pierpont," Grace said. "Handsome Harry. You can be like him. You're really dashing, you know that?"

Calvin didn't say anything.

"Bobby says were going to need to get guns," she said to Calvin. "Buy one for you, one for me."

Grace could have been running around getting the props for the school play.

We're going to need guns, aren't we? We have to make it look realistic.

Calvin just nodded. He had gotten over the feeling of stepping into quicksand and now found himself embracing the plan.

Calvin had never heard of Harry Pierpont, and he'd never heard himself called dashing.

Grace gave Calvin one of Lydia's business cards from her apartment.

On the back she wrote Mi Casita Motel room 211.

"Two o'clock, no earlier, no later," she said, "knock three times."

Calvin nodded.

Knock three times.

Just like the song.

"This guy," she said, "this guy will sell the guns to you. I could get them myself, but Bobby says it's better if you do it."

She gave Calvin cash and another quick, dry kiss.

She smiled at him.

"That's for now," she said, "there's more where that came from."

BAD COMPANY

Bad Company felt like shit.

Which made no difference to anyone but him.

Nobody really knew the real Raymond "Bad Company" Moore.

Most people didn't even know his name was Raymond Moore.

Bad Company kept his real name kind of a secret.

All people knew were the obvious things. You get out of line in the bar? You end up with an arm from Bad Company in the middle of your face.

You're gonna hit the floor and you're gonna remember how you got there.

Nobody knew the real Bad Company, though, not really.

Bad Company liked things that way just fine.

First, people saw his hands.

BAD COMPANY across his knuckles.

Olde English lettering, and just enough fingers to spell the two words out.

The thumbs were tricky, but he'd figured it out.

He'd gotten a tattoo artist in Glendale to do the job. Bad Company nearly took the tattoo artist's head off when he asked if Bad Company was getting the tattoo on account of the band. He only restrained himself because he knew the guy could do a half decent job on hands, which wasn't as easy as it looked.

He'd seen a guy who had *LOVE* and *HATE* spelled out across his knucks.

Somebody had tattooed them upside down. That kind of sloppiness pissed Bad Company off, because he was also an artist, just like the guy with the needles and ink, and Bad Company didn't like half-assed effort.

Bad Company used cans of spray paint for his art. He could take four or five cans and make a design you wouldn't believe on the side of a railroad freight car. Designs with bubbles were his specialties. The bubbles always got you.

The bubbles were real as hell.

Bad Company had been drinking gin and beer last night.

This time of year, the van was perfect. The Econoline was a prize. The Econoline got hot in the summer, there was no use in denying it, but Bad Company was a desert rat. Even though he didn't particularly like it, Bad Company was used to the heat.

In the summer, he didn't sleep inside the van.

At night, after the Horse closed, Bad Company crawled under the Econoline where he kept his bedroll. People worried about snakes, but Bad Company figured if you didn't mess with them, they wouldn't mess with you.

This time of year though, was cold. Even in the desert, when the sun went down, you could freeze .

The Econoline was his little casita, and Bad Company was glad he had won it.

The plates were fine, as long as he didn't take unusual risks.

Bad Company won the Econoline fair and square from an Okie shit-kicker at Slab City.

What the hell was it about people made them so sure of themselves when it came to dice? Dice weren't even one of Bad Company's specialties, but he'd still been able to beat the shit-kicker out of all of his money.

The man insisted upon a chance to win his money back. They'd rolled for his van, and Bad Company used his own Golden Nugget dice.

He won the van fair and square. Too damned bad the man didn't like it.

Bad Company didn't like losing any more than anyone else did. He understood the man's feelings, but even after Bad Company gave him a chance to earn his money back, the man had lost again.

* * *

The problem for the Okie shit-kicker was his mouth.

He'd bragged all evening about the job he'd had in Laughlin, something involving refrigeration. He made no friends around the campfire.

Then, it turned out the shit-kicker was a poor loser.

Bitching and moaning while turning over the keys to Bad Company, the shit-kicker wrote out a poorly spelled title transfer to Bad Company by the light of the campfire. Bad Company had dated a legal secretary and he knew the importance of a clean paper trail.

After grabbing the title, Bad Company jumped in the van and drove through the maze of school busses, tepees, motor homes and lean-tos, out of Slab City.

Into the clear desert.

He drove north through the early morning hours before stopping in Barstow to buy enough spray paint to change the van from mostly white to olive green. Bad Company decided to return to Tucson rather than continuing up the coast.

The paint job would look military enough to get him at least into Arizona.

In Tucson, Bad Company landed a job as a bouncer at the Crazy Horse. It wasn't difficult for Bad Company to get the job. Nobody wanted to mess with Bad Company.

The shit-kicker had fitted the van out nice with a Coleman propane stove and a couple ice coolers. For all his talk, the shit-kicker knew what he was doing when it came to air conditioning. The van maintained a comfortable temperature while the motor was running.

Bad Company knew he would have to get new license plates before he went on any trips outside Tucson. He was also going to do something about the bed which was really no bed at all, just a shabby pile of dirty sheets twisted in the back.

Maybe one of those waterbeds would work in the van. He wondered about the idea.

He'd crashed on a waterbed when he had gone through Yuma and almost hadn't gotten out of the house before the owners got home.

The waterbed had been nice.

There were signs for a waterbed place on billboards all over Tucson. Signs with the same blonde you'd see on the television ads.

What the hell? The idea of the waterbed in the van might just work. The van looked like there was pretty good suspension underneath. If the load was too much and the van couldn't handle the weight of the waterbed, Bad Company figured he could just keep the vehicle as a crash pad while he was still in Tucson and then he could sell the thing to somebody when he decided to leave town.

But he wasn't leaving yet.

He had his job at the Crazy Horse.

And then there was this bank job.

Indirectly, the Econoline had led to the first meeting between Bad Company and Big Bobby Phillips.

It wasn't the first time Bad Company had seen Big Bobby. The first time Bad Company saw Bobby was up in Black Canyon City, and they hadn't spoken to one another. As far as Bad Company knew, Big Bobby hadn't even seen him up there. Bobby had been pretty busy.

Bobby Phillips had come into the Crazy Horse and started talking to Bad Company. Bad Company had noticed the tan, the hair, the iron cross.

The line of shit a mile long about his background in the ski towns of Colorado.

Bad Company meant to ask him about Black Canyon City, but Big Bobby was already pitching the idea of the bank job to Bad Company.

The bank job sounded good.

A nice even split among the team. Bobby was always talking about the team, like he was the general manager of the Dodgers.

Then Bobby got down to some specifics.

"You're gonna need to cover those tattoos when we do the job," Bobby said.

Bad Company just looked at him. Who did this guy think he was dealing with? Bad Company knew which end was up. He would be wearing coveralls and some gloves, wouldn't he?

Bobby Phillips would have made a hell of a salesman. He could talk you into something before you knew it and he had convinced Bad Company.

Bad Company would be there for the intimidation factor, naturally.

"You're the first guy they see. They see you, it's ballgame, right?"

In Bad Company's mind, it worked out to a win-win, situation. The best kind.

A no-brainer.

The funny thing about Bobby was, he didn't drive. He didn't drive *at all*. Maybe he'd been in prison too long. All that ski-bum shit he talked about? You could tell Bobby was a con.

The thing about the driving was funny. Who the hell doesn't drive?

Bobby always had a lady, and they were always good-looking and young. They drove him around like they were in some James Bond movie. That's how good looking they were.

Bad Company closed his eyes then opened them again.

Gin and beer.

That's what he'd been drinking last night.

That's why he felt like shit.

Gin and beer was a leftover habit from when he had still been riding his scoot.

He'd started drinking it after he saw Big Bobby Phillips the first time.

The waitress at the place in Black Canyon City had brought him a beer when he'd come in, hot and sweaty from the ride from Phoenix. Even though it hadn't been too hot that day, Bad Company had been hot enough.

Bad Company remembered Black Canyon City.

This was a couple of a year ago, right?

He was on his own, on his scoot.

He planned to camp near Oak Creek or Sedona. Up there where there's so many stars the night sky is practically white. All that shit.

He stopped at the steak house in Black Canyon City. The place made a big deal about Rocky Mountain oysters. The waitress offered them to Bad Company and he'd shaken his head no.

Bad Company ordered a steak well done.

Baked potato side. Salad bar.

He wasn't eating gonads.

Bad Company had never seen Big Bobby Phillips before the night at the Black Canyon Steak House.

Even up in Black Canyon Bobby wore the shorts and the ski shades.

You wouldn't guess Bobby was good with women, looking at him with his tubby little body and his long gray hair, but he always had one around. That night at Black Canyon City, the woman Bobby was with looked like Angie Dickinson.

Not the Angie Dickinson from *Big Bad Mama.*

Before that, back from the early days. The woman was Bobby's driver, of course.

Bad Company had watched Bobby drinking Jack Daniels, laughing about something stupid.

There was a whole gang around him. Who knows what they were up to? Maybe they had just finished a bank job.

There was a dancer on a stage next to the bar. She was just going through the motions. She was doing something with a cowboy hat like she was Chita Rivera.

Ho hum.

You think you get top dance talent in Black

Canyon City?

Guess again.

The woman who looked like Angie Dickinson had been sitting next to Bobby at the bar and Bobby hadn't been paying a damn bit of attention to her.

Bad Company was watching.

Bad Company couldn't have cared any less about the dancer because Bobby's girlfriend was a hell of a lot sexier than the woman up there on the stage, and Bobby was busy not paying attention to her.

Bobby's girlfriend looked bored and maybe a little put-out.

Bad Company remembered thinking maybe he should say something to her.

To hell with with this guy, right?

Next thing you know, Bobby's standing up and waving his arms around. The dancer stopped with the cowboy hat. She got off the top of the stage and started to cover up her chest like the place was getting raided.

One of the guys with Bobby was sprawled out on the floor like he'd had a heart attack. People were running around, trying to decide if they needed to do CPR or a Heimlich maneuver.

Bad Company glanced at the guy on the floor and could see the guy was dead.

Bobby Phillips still holding his Jack.

One guy kept saying they were going to need to have a Viking funeral.

"You know," the guy said. "We lay him out real

nice out in the desert next to his bike. Pile wood around him and pour on some gas and then torch him. That's what he would want."

Bad Company heard a few people agreeing.

He knew he had to get out of there.

Then Bad Company heard Bobby Phillip's voice.

"What kind of shit idea is that?" Bobby said.

Bobby had been right.

The idea of a Viking funeral was stupid.

Even though they were far from the city, you start a bonfire like that, cops are going to come in and ask questions. Bad Company wasn't sure what the penalty was for unlicensed cremation and he didn't want to find out.

Bobby's girlfriend had disappeared.

Now, Bad Company knew she had probably just been getting her car, but that night, Bad Company thought maybe he could catch up with the woman in the parking lot.

Maybe she would want to smoke some reefer.

Bad Company remembered regretting not following her.

Getting her away from Big Bobby.

Instead, Bad Company had ridden his bike all the way from Black Canyon City to a bar in Catalina.

The waitress in Catalina plopped a beer in front of Bad Company and asked him if he needed anything with it.

Right then, the idea of gin and beer came to Bad Company.

The waitress probably meant did he want French

fries or a pickled egg, but Bad Company told the waitress he wanted a shot of gin right down the side of his beer.

He'd pointed into the top of the glass like he'd done it a hundred times and told her he wanted it down the side so it didn't mess with the foam any.

Bad Company never had gin in his beer before, but he damn near had it every time after.

SEMMERLING LM4

The man was waiting for Calvin in the scroungy motel room.

Before he took the weapons out of the big Samsonite suitcases in the Mi Casita motel room, Calvin looked at him.

He was short, all right.

So what? Calvin didn't have anything against short people, but caution was another one of Calvin's habits.

Checking the man out wasn't something Grace told him to do.

Calvin just knew.

Watch the person, not the object. You learn that, don't you? It doesn't matter whether you're playing cards or getting your car washed. You watch the person.

Calvin was watching to make sure the man selling the guns took him seriously.

The man wasn't *just* short, he was small.

Small hands, small neck, small ears. Very small

ears. Mouse ears. Not like Mickey, more like a real live mouse. He'd probably had a hell of a time lugging the Samsonites up the stairs.

None of Calvin's concern, but he wondered about it.

This was a temporary meeting space, a pay-by-the-hour motel on Miracle Mile. Calvin had his shades on, not wanting anybody to get the wrong idea about him meeting this man here in this motel. Not that there was anyone in the place except the dude behind the desk.

The man with the suitcases had unchained the door and motioned when Calvin knocked. A big hurry-up sign like he had to catch a plane in the next few minutes.

The man with the suitcases hadn't touched anything in the room. Maybe he'd made a deal at the front desk. Even the drinking glasses in the motel room still retained their sanitary seals. Walking by the glasses, Calvin flicked the top of one of the them with the middle finger of his right hand like he was tuning a kettle drum. The man glared at him but didn't say anything.

It was important this man give Calvin his due respect and not treat Calvin casually.

Plus, somewhere, he should have heard the customer is always right, and Calvin was the customer.

Calvin had good money to spend on these guns, and he didn't plan to get treated like he himself wasn't serious.

Calvin pointed to the bathroom.

"Mind I take a leak in there?" he said.

"Suit yourself," the man said. "Don't use the towels"

At first, it looked like the man was only willing to open one of the suitcases.

"Practical items, all of these," the man said. "Pieces you're going to want for anything you got in mind."

"I got nothing in mind," Calvin said, "just go ahead and show me 'em."

Watching the man's eyes and hands making carnival passes over the guns. Droopy eyes with bags under them. The man's eyes looked funny in his doll's head skull.

The man carried a long box of Tiparillo cigars in the pocket of his yellow poly shirt. Couple of daddy-o rings on his fingers, onyx with a silver horsehead on one of them, the other one a diamond horseshoe. Kind of Roy Rogers showy.

"What I'm going to display here is what I got today," he said. "I'm getting more items soon. You see something you like here, we make a deal. You want something special you have to wait. Just letting you know ahead of time, these here got no record, nothing. They don't exist."

"What's that horsehead?" Calvin said.

He pointed at the ring on the man's right hand.

"What are you talking about?" the man said.

He lifted his head and looked at Calvin.

Calvin was grinning. Pointing at the ring.

"You're a jockey, or what?"

The man shook his head. He started to put the guns back in the case.

"I don't work with that kind of a comment," he said, "I don't work with that kind of comment at all."

Calvin held up both his hands palms forward.

"Forget it," Calvin said. "I got some guys, some friends I know, not personal friends, but I know them. They happen to be in the racetrack industry. I thought about getting in that line myself at one point. Of course, I wouldn't have been a rider on account of my size."

The man looked satisfied. He didn't look happy, exactly, but he looked satisfied. He patted the handle of the other Samsonite.

"Show me the other one," Calvin said.

"Show me you got cash," the man said.

He wore a Smith and Wesson tucked into a side holster way up level with his belly button. Thin hair. Clenching one of the cigars in his teeth while heaving the second Samsonite up onto the bed.

Both Samsonites were maroon.

"Nice suitcases," Calvin said. "They take a beating, right? They drop 'em from balconies, put 'em in a cage with a gorilla, right? They stay nice."

The man didn't respond. He looked at Calvin again for a few seconds before saying anything.

"You got cash, or what?"

Calvin didn't like it, but it was the man's play. He pulled the bills from his unsnapped shirt pocket.

Tossed them out on the quilted bedspread like he didn't give a shit.

The man squinted and nodded. Snapped open the first Samsonite and then the second.

"Everything I got, they're not exotic. I give you a reasonable amount of ammo to get you started. Should keep you busy, you like to target shoot or whatnot. You can get more anywhere if you're careful."

Ammo he said.

Like some black and white war movie.

Hey Joe, get some more ammo.

The man brought out a Mossberg which was impressive, but not what Calvin had in mind.

He had a 1911, pimped out with pearl handles. The handles were not impressive, at least not to Calvin.

A long barreled Dirty Harry .357 Magnum. That was a possibility, although Calvin hated thinking about being compared to fuzz.

Another nondescript shotgun, cheaper than the Mossberg.

Calvin shook his head no.

Then Calvin picked up a tiny pistol from the bed. About the size of his palm. Wooden grips.

"The Semmerling LM4, the man said. "*Not* semi-auto, though. You like it? If you do, you got good taste. It ain't cheap, either. Those grips? Cocobolo."

Calvin nodded, then put it down.

Cocobolo? What the shit?

Calvin pointed to a gun the man had taken out

61

last, like it was an afterthought. This gun made his pulse race.

A grease gun. Like on *Combat!* and *Rat Patrol*.

"M3, technically an M3A1. Fires forty-five caliber, just like a Thompson machine gun. Lots of fun if you're an enthusiast."

Calvin Gamble picked it up. Somebody had added a wooden stock, but it was the same gun they'd been using since what, Guadalcanal?

That black and white war movie again.

Hey Joe, bring me the grease gun while you're getting the ammo.

"I'll take this one," Calvin said, then pointed at the Semmerling. It could come in handy. "I'll go ahead and take that one too."

As soon as he'd seen the grease gun, a plan came into Calvin's head. Better than anything Bobby Phillips could come up with, either. Calvin had shot rats at the dump back home when he was a kid. He had been quick, even with an old bolt action. With the grease gun?

Calvin would be like lightning.

He knew all about taping the clips together, he'd seen Lee Marvin in *The Dirty Dozen*.

Let's go get those Krauts.

"I'll take all the ammo you got on hand for this baby," Calvin said.

Grace and Calvin were going to a lot of trouble for this job.

She was driving and he was buying the guns.

If Grace and Calvin got caught with the stolen

car or the guns, they would be facing prison time.

So, why shouldn't they keep *all* the money from the bank job?

With that kind of cash Calvin and Grace could go to Mexico and live like a king and a queen.

All they needed was nerve and a plan. Calvin couldn't wait to share his idea with Grace.

"I'll wrap 'em up for you no sweat," the man said. "Nice thing is the two of them fire the same kinda ammo. On account of that, you don't need to get hung up figuring things out."

He pointed at the Semmerling.

"You believe that baby spits out forty-fives? Crazy, right? Just watch your fingers. That's a shorty."

Calvin Gamble picked up the Semmerling and held it with the barrel pointing toward the popcorn ceiling of the motel room.

"By the way, that ain't fully auto. You gotta advance the lever each shot. Probably want to check that out a few times."

Calvin wasn't listening to him. He was looking at the Semmerling.

"Yeah, crazy," Calvin said. "It's dang near unbelievable.

Calvin was thinking about his new plan.

Glad he'd met Grace

Meeting Grace was meant to be.

Like stars aligning.

Something like that.

He was going to be something. The *two of them*

were going to be something.
No more penny-ante burglaries.
Calvin would be hitting the big-time.
He paid for the guns and left.

HIP-HUGGERS

Grace didn't give Calvin any static about the new plan.

"I've gone out and worked that grease gun, Grace," he said. "Took it out in the boonies and put a bunch of rounds through the thing. I got it down."

She was impressed by his initiative. She listened to him, staring at him with the big blue eyes she used in the waterbed ads.

Waited until he was finished.

"So, we keep the money, that's what you're saying, Bud?"

Calvin nodded.

"We keep it all, Grace. Then maybe we go to Mexico until things kinda cool down. Maybe a cruise."

"Mexico," Grace said. "You and me, Bud?"

"Just you and me, Grace," he said. "Why not? We're putting ourselves out on the line here, aren't we?"

Calvin liked the way the smile crept onto Grace's face. She looked like a cat getting ready for milk.

"Why should we let this dude take all the

money?" Calvin said. "Seems like if we take it, nobody's the wiser, and the trail ends up there. What's the place you said?"

"I didn't say," Grace said. "But it's up near Catalina. You know where that is? You head up Oracle and you end up in the middle of nowhere."

As if Calvin didn't know where Catalina was.

"Sounds perfect," he said. "We make it look like a drug deal gone bad. You read about those in the papers all the time. No shit, it sounds perfect. Why not?"

"Bud," she said, "you may be on to something, you know?"

She wore white hip-huggers and a purple halter top.

The way she lay across the bed reminded him of the waterbed ads.

"You ever sleep in one of those waterbeds?" he said.

Grace shook her head. She hadn't even heard his question.

Grace had gotten turned on when she saw the guns he had bought on Miracle Mile and she definitely liked the idea of keeping all the money.

Calvin could see by the look on her face and the way she was treating him.

Calvin knew a lot of women got turned on by guns.

He'd read an article about it once getting his hair cut.

Why Women Date Cops.

Grace must be one of those women.

Grace gave him a sexy look.

Maybe she didn't expect Calvin to think for himself.

She wouldn't have been the first to underestimate him .

Calvin had been a successful burglar for years before meeting Grace.

He was already a pro.

You get more than you bargain for with Calvin Gamble.

RING MY BELL

The clock radio awakened her.

You can ring my bell, ring my bell.

Grace Partridge felt an adrenalin surge. She liked the feeling. Her blood quickening its pace. The surging to her head.

This was Thursday morning.

It's showtime, folks.

She loved the lightheaded, weightless feeling of action when a plan was in place.

She was on a roller coaster going skyward. The part where you look around, see how high you're going, and you just don't care. You don't think about the flimsy track beneath you. The only thing on your mind is the freefall ahead.

Grace looked at herself in the mirror. Even in the morning she looked good.

Things were going as well as she could hope.

Having Calvin Gamble think he'd come up with the idea was nice. Grace loved the way he'd brought it up, like he had to convince her.

"Do you like the plan?" he said.

She looked at him like it was a new idea and she had to think it over.

"Wow," she said.

Like Calvin Gamble was some kind of genius.

"Bud, that's amazing. Like, we take the money?"

She put on good clothes. Dark, conservative. Something Lydia would have worn, but sexy. Good make-up, but different from when she was meeting men.

You can ring my bell, ring my bell.

High heels definitely. You need to make an impression, right?

My bell, ding-a-ling-a-ling.

Grace had worked at Old Tucson. She had played the part of a dance hall girl in three easily forgotten episodes of a television western. The job hadn't led to anything. Grace's lines? Nothing.

Come on Johnny, have a heart.

Those kinds of lines.

But Grace got a good look at the female star. A silver-haired actress in the twilight of her career. Grace watched her. Along with the silver hair, the actress had a sultry voice and a reputation.

Nothing Grace didn't have.

Just the breaks.

Three lousy episodes.

Come on Johnny, have a heart.

Grace got checks for the reruns, but she never watched the episodes.

The jealous bitch got Grace fired.

My bell.

Ding-a-ling-a-ling.

BIG BOBBY

Big Bobby stood outside the efficiency apartment he called home. The place was a rent-by-the-week brown-and-serve around the corner from the Lamplighter Bar. It was still early in the morning. The sun was rising and there was nobody on Big Bobby's street when Calvin and Grace pulled up in the Chevette.

"This is where he lives?" Calvin said. "I was expecting something a little snazzier. You said he was a mastermind."

"Never mind that, Bud," Grace said. "He's a genius in his own way. We won't worry about that, though."

She squeezed his bootcut jeans above his knee.

"You're going to have to sit in the back, though," she said. "He's gonna want to be up front with me."

"That's fine," Calvin said. "I'll keep my eye on him, though. He looks a little shifty."

Big Bobby Phillips was probably five inches shorter than Calvin. His thick upper body was mostly covered by a guayabera which left his gut hanging over a pair of Ocean Pacific surf shorts.

Flip-flops over his spindly legs.

Bobby looked like a pony keg propped on a piano stool.

Holding a Big Gulp in one hand and a duffel bag in the other.

Big Bobby Phillips took tanning *seriously.*

White aviator shades.

Big Bobby looked like a hangover but was all business when he got in the car.

He looked at Grace, checked his Casio.

Shook his head.

"Late."

Calvin checked his Timex.

"Not by my watch," he said.

Calvin trying to be helpful.

At least accurate.

Big Bobby Phillips shook his head. Looked over the seat. Calvin smirked and gave him a three fingered wave

Phillips looked back at Grace. Pointed back at Calvin.

"Who the hell is this?"

"He's coming with us, Bobby," Grace said. "He's the second gun."

"Second gun?" Big Bobby said. "What the hell is second gun supposed to mean?"

Calvin smiled at Big Bobby.

"I'm helping you, Bob," Calvin said. "By the way, that's a hell of a tan you got. Looks like mahogany."

"You aren't coming," Big Bobby said.

He looked at Grace.

"He's not coming."

Grace smiled.

"You have another driver, Bobby?"

OUTLAWS

Bad Company watched Chemo and Albatross taking turns throwing knives at the side of the abandoned trailer near Catalina. Keeping score like they were playing a game of horse. Backs turned, between the legs, over the shoulder. Early evening there was color stretching across the sky. Waiting for Big Bobby and the money.

Neither Chemo nor Albatross knew shit about knives.

"That ain't the way you hold it," Albatross said.

He moved toward Chemo.

"Let me show you something."

Chemo pulled away from Albatross like he was guarding his food.

"Like you know anything about throwing, man," he said. "What you gotta do is you gotta hold onto the blade a second longer than you think. That's what gives it the spin. *English*, right? That's what you gotta do."

The spin accounted for Chemo's knife clattering against the wall and sliding down onto the caliche next to the wall of the trailer.

He was miserable. Bad Company hated watching

these two.

Much longer than this, the sun would be completely down, and there was no guarantee Bobby would even have gotten out here by then.

But Bobby called the shots.

Big Bobby Phillips had the cash and he made the rules.

He'd be here, eventually.

Bad Company knew enough not to join in the game being played by Albatross and Chemo. Better to watch. Playing horse like this? You shitting me? With a basketball, for sure.

Bad Company was six foot six and he could still hoop. He'd shoot baskets for money any day with these clowns. Bad Company could hit three point shots from the baseline, no sweat. Dunk with either hand.

Throwing knives? These guys were like children.

Chemo and Albatross were more or less aiming at the trailer. They might be able to hit its broad side, but they weren't skilled. They kept messing around, changing their grips, shouting like Tarzan of the Apes, missing the mark each time they threw.

Plus they weren't getting tired of the game.

Bad Company was sick and tired of watching them but he had to wait for the same reason they were waiting.

You're waiting for the kind of money you get from a job like this, you stick around.

Bad Company could see Chemo was fidgety.

Whatever Chemo smoked on the ride up from Casas Adobes was beginning to wear off.

The job had gone smoothly in spite of these two, and in spite of the other guy.

Bobby would get here soon with the cash.

Bobby's jobs were good, and they were getting better. Nobody wanted to piss off Bobby, not even Chemo.

Chemo was a prick. Bad Company knew it as soon as they met.

"Righteous name," Chemo said to Bad Company. "Like the band."

Bad Company didn't even straighten him out. He didn't even tell the asshole he'd gotten his name years before the band came on the scene.

Not saying he didn't like the band.

That wasn't the point.

"Watch this."

Albatross wheezed instead of speaking, but Bad Company heard him this time. Albatross was shouting to Chemo. Bad Company heard Albatross's knife clatter down the side of the trailer.

They weren't using the right tools.

Albatross's hunting knife might look threatening strapped on his belt when he entered a Circle K, but it wasn't a throwing knife. Neither was the knock-off KA-BAR Chemo bought at the swap meet.

These two were second-raters.

Part of Big Bobby's genius was nobody got

friendly with anybody else.

Bad Company sure as hell wasn't going to make friends with these guys.

After they split the money, they would all go their separate ways until the next time.

The shack was out in the scrub desert between Catalina and Oracle. Somebody had started clearing the land with a bulldozer then changed their mind halfway through.

All the bulldozer left was a derelict Aristocrat trailer, shot with bullet holes. Roof gone. Open to the elements.

Bobby said he knew the guy who owned it but Bad Company suspected that was just part of Bobby's bullshit.

REGULAR BOY SCOUTS

It was almost dark. Big Bobby still hadn't shown up with the money.

The split should have occurred before this.

This ritual was making Bad Company angrier.

Chemo and Albatross had taken a break from throwing knives. They started a fire with mesquite branches piled against creosote-soaked railroad ties.

They were regular Boy Scouts, these two. This was a good time to set a fire in the desert. A good time to attract the sheriff department.

Chemo, with the American flag bandanna wrapped around his head, looked like Pigpen from the Dead.

Albatross, as tall as Bad Company, was albino. His white arms were criss-crossed by dark India ink tattoos. Dice, swords, skulls. Albatross specialized in electronics. He could wire anything.

The blaze was fierce. Bad Company stood with Chemo and Albatross watching the sparks push their way into the night sky. He decided to walk back to his Econoline.

He would wait there.

The Econoline was parked away from the trailer and next to the arroyo.

Bad Company couldn't hear the clatter of knives any more and he was no longer within the bonfire's light.

LIKE THE BAND

Bad Company knew a couple of things.

He had reached the Econoline and had opened the van's front door. Far enough from the fire he couldn't hear them anymore.

Albatross and Chemo knew as much as Bad Company.

There was a lot of money to split.

When it came to getting their share of the cash, each of them were going to have to look out for their own interests.

"The money is gonna be safe and sound," Big Bobby said. "Right in the trunk of the car with me and Grace."

The other guy smiled.

Bobby said the guy's name was Bud.

"You heard him," Bud said. "It'll be safe as milk, bro."

When Bad Company saw Bud, he had almost backed out. He'd seen this fuck-up before at the Crazy Horse. Bad Company didn't like him and he didn't want to work with him. A fuck-up like Bud could get you killed for no reason whatsoever.

The woman must have pressured Bobby to

include Bud in on the plan. Probably to get more than her share.

Greedy bitch.

She was driving Bobby.

Bad Company had to hand it to Big Bobby. The sucker knew how to plan a job.

Bobby was a freak about research.

Bobby had taken the Sun Tran and watched the bank for weeks. He knew the manager's name. He knew when the manager came in. Knew when the first teller showed up. The manager, Gerald Quincy was always a couple minutes earlier than the Dudley Do-Right-looking teller who always came in a few minutes after Quincy.

Chemo and Bad Company had gone in first, masks on, reaching the manager just before he'd turned on the Mr. Coffee in the break room.

After, Chemo reached around and put the gun to Quincy's head and got him to open the vault. There was a lot more money than they had expected. The bank served as a depository for three other branches.

They were all going to get plenty of cash.

They had loaded the duffel bag full.

But the duffel bag was *all* they were going to get. The bank manager didn't have access to the inner vault.

From the way he was hyperventilating, you could tell Quincy was telling the truth.

The money didn't upset Bad Company. Even without the inner vault, this was a hell of a payday.

Bad Company wasn't even sure if Bobby knew how to drive. That was another one of the things about him. Bobby always had a lady driver and the lady driver always looked nice.

Bad Company shook his head.

This driver was way more than nice looking.

Before she put on her mask, Bad Company thought again how much she looked like Samantha on *Bewitched*. Blonde hair and a nose she could probably twitch.

Unlike the women in the Bond movies, though, she wasn't driving a fancy car. This woman was driving a nondescript beige Chevette. Just what Bobby wanted.

Albatross had lifted it for Bobby from the El Con Mall and gotten plates south of Broadway.

"You need a muscle car for your getaway, you aren't doing it right," Bobby said. "You think driving something like a GTO full speed isn't going to attract attention? What you need is plain Jane all the way."

Albatross cut the alarm and phone lines at the bank. The place would be a tomb after the team left until customers started pounding on the doors at opening time.

Ten o'clock.

By then, the team would be down the road.

Chemo and Bad Company put Quincy and Dudley Do-Right in the vault with their mouths, wrists and ankles duct taped before walking out of the bank.

Chemo drove his own Matador across to Golf Links where he'd dropped Bad Company at his Econoline. Bad Company had parked the van near a drive-in taqueria.

Bad Company had started to notice he was hungry on the cross-town drive. Rather than head immediately to Catalina, he'd driven to the taqueria and ordered a pescado burro from a waitress who came out wearing orange hotpants. Her nametag said Veronica.

"Here you go," she said. She handed him the bag and counted out the change. He'd paid with a twenty.

Veronica looked at the tattoos across Bad Company's knuckles.

"Bad Company?" she said. "Like the band?"

She looked at him a little more closely. Pushed the change toward him.

"Like the band," Bad Company said.

Her eyes widened.

"You know what?" Bad Company said. "Go ahead and keep the change."

COPACETIC

Bad Company looked out the window of the Econoline in Catalina. The fire was enormous now. Still no sign of Bobby and the other two.

Maybe they got pulled over.

If that happened, Bad Company would get nothing from this heist.

Should he have trusted Bobby? Maybe he should have insisted on going in the same vehicle as the money.

If Bad Company had to trust someone in this crew, he figured he would trust Bobby.

Bad Company didn't trust Bud for a second.

Bobby wouldn't trust Bud either.

It was an elaborate system Bobby worked out based on the principle of mutual mistrust. Following the plan, each participant would get their share of the take. The plan was as close as you could get to honor among thieves.

Some things Bad Company had no control over. If the cash was in the trunk of the car, neither Bobby nor Bud could mess with it.

Bobby had planned this job perfectly, but he'd let the woman steer him into a bad decision.

Bad Company didn't like that at all.

Bad Company was sure the woman had gotten Bud involved in the plan. Bud hadn't worked his way into Bobby's favor this quickly. Bringing Bud along with her meant the woman was not trustworthy.

"We needed one more gun to do this thing," Bobby said.

He wanted insurance in case somebody came in the bank at the wrong moment.

"This guy is solid," Bobby said. "Nothing to worry about."

Bad Company hated it when people said there was nothing to worry about because there was always *something* to worry about, especially on a bank job.

And Bud sure as hell wasn't *solid*.

This guy Bud had even been a problem at the Crazy Horse.

Bud was a creep. Bad Company had thrown him out a couple of weeks ago for messing with some of the ladies near the bull machine.

Bobby had gotten *this* guy? *Bud* was the best he could get?

Bad Company went over the events of the robbery in his head. Bud hadn't wasted any time before he started causing problems.

Bad Company went into the bank first. Just like Bobby planned.

Bad Company grabbed the bank manager.

The guy didn't make a fuss.

The bank manager, Quincy, wasn't causing problems, but Bud came in and started pushing him around just for the hell of it.

Like the guy could produce more money out of thin air if Bud acted tough.

Bud had a gun pointed at the guy's head.

The manager was nervous and who could blame him?

Bad Company knew there was trouble when Bud showed up with the damn grease gun.

This was a bank job and Bud thought he was on *Rat Patrol*.

"You aren't holding out on us, are you?" Bud said to the bank manager.

"There's rolled coins," Quincy said, "You want those?"

The bank manager was nervous.

Who wouldn't be? He wasn't thinking about what he was saying.

He sure as *hell* wasn't holding out on them.

"Coins?" Bud said, "You think we're here for coins?"

Bud pushed the grease gun up under the manager's septum.

Bad Company was pissed.

No need for this kind of thing to happen when the guy was cooperating.

Bud was showboating.

The manager wasn't thinking. He hadn't thought about how useless coins were to these guys.

If the manager were killed, and it *could* have happened, law enforcement's concern would raise to maximum.

Murder one, Jack.

Intentional.

There's no coming back, even if the prosecutors can't put the murder weapon in your hands right away. They keep digging around until they do.

Bobby hadn't seen this part. He'd been with the tellers.

Dudley Do-Right lived up to his name.

He did the right thing.

Stood to the side and watched.

Made no more comments.

Everything was copacetic.

Bad Company watched Bobby Phillips stuff money into the duffel bag then into the back of the Chevette.

They would count but Bad Company made a guess.

More money than they expected.

Bud was an asshole, but the job got done.

Bad Company wouldn't work with him again.

In Catalina, Bad Company parked the van away from the trailer.

Out of sight.

He was the first to arrive.

The other two vehicles hadn't gotten there yet.

Bad Company walked to the trailer. His work boots made heavy tracks in the sand.

Bobby had a few folding chairs outside the place.

Bleached aluminum and threadbare canvas.

Bad Company sat down to wait. Reached deep into his vest pocket and pulled out a decent-sized doobie made from two Zig-Zag papers.

Rolled the joint through his fingers like he was doing close-up magic.

A woman living up on North First in a sandy stucco apartment complex said Bad Company looked like the man on the Zig-Zag cigarette papers on account of the beard and the bandanna Bad Company sometimes wore on his head.

Bad Company liked that, sort of.

He liked the lady, anyway. He figured he could capitalize on the resemblance so he got a fierce Zig-Zag man tattoo on his right arm.

When he went to show the woman it turned out she'd moved.

The people at the complex where she lived didn't know where she went.

She had been living in apartment number seven.

The guy living there now looked like a grad student. He blocked the door so Bad Company couldn't see past him.

The grad student didn't wanted Bad Company to see his girlfriend, but that didn't work. Bad Company had already seen her.

She wasn't the woman who said Bad Company looked like the Zig-Zag man.

The guy blocking the door didn't think much about Bad Company's new tattoo when Bad Company showed it to him.

The guy shrugged. Asked Bad Company if he knew the Zig-Zag man was modeled after a Zouave soldier from North Africa.

"They were Algerians, did you know that?"

Bad Company shook his head no.

The guy gave a look.

Of course you wouldn't know that.

"They fought with the French," he said. "Of course there were some Zouave regiments in the Civil War, too."

"No shit," Bad Company said. "Who the fuck doesn't know that?"

The guy said Bad Company should keep the tattoo clean while it was new.

"Those things start festering after a while if you don't take care of them," the guy said.

He took a little poke with his index finger toward Bad Company's arm.

"They get infected easy. Looks like it's already getting a little screwed up around the side there. Probably could use a little attention."

Bad Company looked. There wasn't anything wrong with his tattoo. The guy was just messing with him, maybe.

"Right there," the guy said.

Pointed a little closer.

Bad Company took a closer at the tattoo which he'd kept covered with Vaseline.

Sure enough, the tattoo wasn't quite right.

The Zig-Zag man's eye wasn't right and never would be.

Bad Company knew there was no fixing it.

What the hell was wrong with the guy, though? Bad Company had just showed up at the door to find a woman who wasn't living there anymore. He wasn't looking for a history lesson or for a hygiene lecture either, for that matter.

What made the grad student think Bad Company didn't know how to take care of a new tattoo?

The screwed-up eye wasn't the thing that bothered Bad Company most. What bothered him was finding out the Zig-Zag man was from Africa.

Bad Company didn't like having an Arab on his arm.

He didn't like that one bit.

The woman said he looked like the Zig-Zag man was lucky she had moved.

Funny though, Bad Company couldn't remember what she looked like or even her name, but he remembered she lived in apartment number seven.

Bad Company looked up when the Matador pulled in and parked close to the trailer.

He walked down to meet them.

Albatross and Chemo.

Chemo showing up stoned, Albatross the driver.

"Bad Company," Chemo said, "You musta flown."

They hadn't seen his van.

"Where's your ride, bro?" Albatross said.

Bad Company looked at him.

"Like you said. I flew."

It was a long wait.

Big Bobby was dragging his ass.

Bad Company was getting tired watching for the Chevette while watching these two play with their knives.

Bad Company got up. Walked behind the arroyo.

Albatross and Chemo didn't notice.

The hell with this.

He got into the van.

Might as well take a nap.

UNWRITTEN LAWS OF BANK ROBBERY

Bud liked the way Grace looked. She was dressed nice for the job, just like a model in one of those women's magazine articles about making a good first impression. A dark suit with wide lapels.

A string of pearls.

That killed Calvin. A string of pearls like she did this every day of the week.

"Did you see how good Bud did, Bobby?" Grace said.

It was dark, and she was driving the beige Chevette. Beige paint and beige interior. It really wasn't a bad car, and it was unassuming, just like Bobby wanted.

The job had been a success, and Calvin was happy.

Albatross, Chemo, and Bad Company had done their jobs.

Holy shit, what kind of names were those,

anyway?

Grace had introduced Calvin as Bud. He liked the way she said the name real sexy.

This is Bud.

Calvin was already thinking about the next job. He would be the leader next time. He would do a hell of a lot better than Big Bobby Phillips.

Albatross and Chemo were driving to Catalina in one car. Bad Company insisted upon driving himself in his Econoline.

Grace was driving. She was smoking a Virginia Slim and looking over her shoulder at Bobby Phillips.

Bobby did not look happy.

Calvin found this strange. Where was the celebration? They had done a great job.

Maybe there was more he needed to learn about bank robbery.

Maybe there were unwritten laws he didn't know about yet.

Bobby looked at Grace.

"Drive up Campbell," he said. "Go all the way to the top."

Which was a hell of a ways out of the way.

Grace looked at him.

"You sure?" she said.

"Just do it," Bobby said.

At the top of Campbell, the lights of the city stretched out in front of them.

It was a magical sight.

The money was in the duffel bag. Some of the

bills were still in their paper wrappers. Calvin hadn't thought about it much, but there was a world of difference between what you took away from a bank heist and what you took from a burglary.

Banks were orderly places. Everything in its place and accounted for. It was different from going into a house where you were never sure what you were going to find. Sometimes you came away with nothing.

Unlike banks, a lot of people were slobs.

Sometimes people left expensive things scattered around and other times they had things looking like carnival prizes locked up like the crown jewels.

"That business with the grease gun was uncalled for," Bobby said.

He was sitting in the back seat, rubbing the soreness out of his right knee.

Grace had told Calvin Bobby had been a ski bum in Telluride and still had problems with his knee.

"That put the operation at risk," Bobby said.

Like he was a tank commander.

"I thought Bud was magnificent," Grace said.

Calvin Gamble liked the way Grace was calling him Bud.

He turned around and looked at Big Bobby.

"How much you think's in the bags, Bobby?" Calvin said.

Bobby didn't say anything.

"You think it's five figures or six?" Calvin said.

"I'm just asking ballpark."

Bobby leaned forward in the seat, his eyes right in front of Calvin.

"Just asking ballpark, are you?"

Calvin grinned and nodded.

"I won't hold you to it, Bobby. Just a round figure guess."

Bobby shook his head. You could tell Bobby spent a lot of time getting his gray hair just right. Calvin didn't hold this against him. He himself spent a lot of time with hair products. He himself was an Herbal Essence man.

But you could tell, between the hair and the tan, Bobby Phillips took a lot of time in front of the mirror.

Bobby's voice was deep and frightening.

"I don't want to hear another fucking word out of you, Bud."

Calvin turned and looked at the skyline again.

He felt the cocobolo handled Semmerling in his pocket.

Tried to pick out landmarks on the sparkling horizon. The bright lights down there in the middle had to be the university. Airport way to the south, so you couldn't see it. The First National Bank tower downtown you could still see but not the time and temperature at the top.

Bobby got out of the car. He took out his gun and started to point it at Calvin. He put it down for a second and waved toward Grace.

"You," Bobby said to Grace. "You get out here too.

Stand next to your boyfriend."

Bobby was waving his gun between Calvin and Grace like he couldn't decide who to shoot first.

The Semmerling was as loud as anything Calvin had ever fired

Calvin was glad the man at the motel had warned him to watch his fingers. The gun really was short. It would have been a shame to shoot his hand off instead of shooting Big Bobby Phillips but it could have happened if he'd gotten klutzy.

Bobby lay dead next to the Chevette with a bloody crater in his gray hair

Calvin turned to Grace. She was staring at Bobby like she'd never seen a dead body before.

Maybe she hadn't seen one, who could say?

This was a first for Calvin, too.

He was experiencing a lot of firsts, lately.

"You ready to go?" Calvin said.

Grace's eyes were still wide.

"What about him?" she said. "We're just going to leave him out here?

"You bet," Calvin said. "It'll just look like one of them drug deals gone bad."

PANEL VAN

Bad Company was still waiting in the back of the van. He was lying on his back, eyes closed, listening.

It was taking forever for Bobby to get up to Catalina. Bobby must have decided to take his own sweet time on account of having the money in the trunk.

It would be just like Big Bobby to get obstinate in order to show who was in charge.

Outside the van, Albatross and Chemo were still throwing the knives, although with less frequency and fewer exclamations.

The fire had their attention.

These boys loved a bonfire.

Bad Company would be glad to be done with these two, but at least they had served a purpose during the job.

Bud had not.

Bad Company opened his eyes.

He thought of something, and he wondered why it hadn't occurred to him before.

Thinking about the blonde in the waterbed ads.

The driver.

That woman on the billboard had been the driver. Sitting there with her string of pearls. He should have seen it before, but he hadn't.

You don't expect a woman on a television ad to be driving your getaway car, do you?

Why hadn't he seen it was her?

VULTURES

Albatross and Chemo had stopped throwing knives by the time Bad Company heard the car coming.

He had only slept a little, his eyes opening and shutting.

He was thinking.

He got out of the van and looked at the Chevette, parked next to the bonfire. None of them could see him.

Chemo and Albatross had put more of the railroad ties on the fire. The flames created a visual barrier separating Bad Company from the others.

In silhouette, Bad Company saw Bud getting out of the Chevette.

Bad Company knew he would see Bobby pulling the the duffel bag from the trunk of the car.

The woman sat behind the wheel of the Chevette.

Bad Company looked at her. From his angle, he got a good look at her face. He was right. She was definitely the same woman from the ad.

On the ad, she was seductive.

Not now. There was something wrong with the

way she looked.

Bad Company started walking back toward the fire, then stopped.

The flames kept him from being seen so he needed to stay behind them.

There was something very tempting about the situation.

He had a rifle in the van.

He thought about the elements at play. The gun was a bolt action he'd bought when he got to Tucson.

Good for hunting javelina, but for this, the gun was not ideal.

Bad Company thought about the situation. He was an accurate shot and he had the element of surprise on his side.

He could go back and grab the rifle, sight them in and drop them like the three little pigs.

Plus one.

He would fan the bolt with the palm of his hand instead of levering for each shot. Maybe he'd get them all quickly enough. Maybe not even so quickly, but he would drop each one before finishing them.

Whatever amount of cash was in the bag would be his alone.

It was tempting.

All of the bodies would be found, eventually. Partially decomposed, partially torn apart by vultures and coyotes. Bloated by heat.

Bad Company shook his head.

He wouldn't do it.

He thought about it, but he wouldn't do it.

Bad Company watched Bud go back to the car.

Pulling something from the front seat.

Probably the woman handed it to him. Bad Company couldn't be sure.

Bud, Bad Company thought.

This guy was some piece of shit.

The way he'd waved his gun around? Bad Company should have shot him in the bank.

Bud pulled out the same grease gun he'd used. The one he'd held under the bank manager's nose.

Waved it for a second. Signaling.

Bud fired.

Albatross went down in a short burst from the M3.

Chemo, right behind him, dragging himself away good as dead.

It took no time. Bad Company stood behind the fire. He watched.

No time for him to go back into the van and grab the gun.

The blonde woman sat in the driver's seat.

She was smiling.

Albatross and Chemo were dead.

The money was gone.

Something else was the matter.

Bad Company had gotten a good view of everything.

He'd seen Bud gun down Albatross and Chemo.

He'd watched the woman driver.

He hadn't seen Big Bobby Phillips.

Bobby wasn't in the car.

He had to be dead.

Bobby would never have let the bank money out of his sight.

FLY IN THE OINTMENT

They had the money and to hell with everything else.

Bobby would have killed both Grace and Calvin.

Left them up at the top of Campbell.

Grace should have been thanking Calvin but she hadn't said a word.

They were driving back to Tucson with the money still in the bag.

Nobody touched the cash since the job.

There was just one fly in the ointment.

Calvin Gamble worried it like a broken tooth.

It was all well and good, hanging out here on the orange sectional, but Calvin knew both he and Grace faced a potential fatal problem.

The bouncer.

How could Calvin forget that dude?

Same guy told Calvin not to be an asshole.

Bad Company was his name.

Bad Company hadn't shown up in Catalina, but he was still a problem.

Calvin had gone ahead and made a split-second

decision to leave the place.

Afterwards, Grace said he'd done the right thing.

They could have waited all night for the big bastard to show up and then they would have had to divide the money.

Better to have done things the way he did them.

Waiting for Bad Company to show up could have taken all night.

When Calvin mentioned Bad Company to Grace she didn't think he was a problem.

"What are you so worried about?" Grace said. "He's nothing."

But he was worried.

Calvin knew Bad Company was out there somewhere.

It wouldn't take a genius to figure out what happened up there.

Bad Company would have rolled up in his van, gotten out, seen the bodies.

He would figure out what happened.

Bad Company would want his money.

Calvin needed to find Bad Company before Bad Company found him.

CROSSTOWN TRAFFIC

Crosstown traffic on Speedway was crazy Friday morning.

Lydia Partridge wondered why she didn't just get a place to live farther east, closer to work.

Living in the Presidio might be romantic but the drive was murder.

And really, what was so romantic about living alone?

After performing a quick errand, Lydia drove through the Fourth Avenue underpass to Sixth Street. She looked in the rear view mirror of the Datsun, making sure the part in her dark hair was just right.

Lydia still had Trinity's card.

She had put it in the tray where she kept her keys after she got home. That had been a couple of nights ago.

Tuesday night?

Living in another part of town would be wiser. Even though she felt safer after learning how to fire the gun, Lydia knew she would never shoot anyone.

The neighborhood had problems. Break-ins and worse.

Living alone made her vulnerable.

She punched the cigarette lighter and reached for her purse.

Took out a cigarette.

She liked where she lived. So what if the ride was long? She could never live in a place like Grace's apartment.

She had thought about Trinity. Looked at his card a few times.

Investigations?

She should have asked him what kind. It probably wasn't anything like the movies.

Did he wait in his office for women like Lydia to walk in the door?

Lydia found an open parking space on 6th Street and walked across the street to the Eagle Bakery.

Coffee and danish.

She wanted to see Trinity again.

She had hinted, hadn't she?

She didn't want to be obvious, but she could have gotten him to stay at El Charro.

Grace wouldn't have let him get away.

Lydia had given him her card. She had taken his.

Just like at some trade convention.

Maybe she could have been more creative, but she had been preoccupied thinking about Grace.

When *wasn't* she thinking about Grace?

Trinity could help with Grace, but Lydia didn't want Trinity to associate Lydia with Grace and her problems.

It would be nice to only be responsible for herself.

Lydia was tired of taking care of Grace.

DUMPSTER STINK

Bad Company woke up in the Econoline. He was parked in his usual spot behind the Crazy Horse.

There was the usual dumpster stink in the alley.

It took a second before Bad Company remembered what happened last night.

Ripped off.

Bud and the woman had all the money.

Those two wouldn't hesitate sacrificing Bad Company if it meant saving their own hides.

Bad Company had to find them.

For now though, they didn't know he had seen them.

Bad Company felt his stomach. It was beginning to settle. He had thrown up last night sometime.

You gotta be careful with fish.

He needed to think things over, but right now he was hurting. He worked his way out of his sleeping bag.

Bad Company stepped out of the van into the alley to take a leak. Getting back in the van, he took his keys from beneath the visor and pulled out of the alley onto Speedway.

Heading toward Grant.

He would force himself to eat something at Mother Hubbard's.

The woman on the billboard.

Big Bobby's driver.

Lying up on a waterbed.

Smiling.

Bad Company knew how to find her.

MOTHER HUBBARD'S

The waitress at Mother Hubbard's knew enough to leave Bad Company alone.

He was drinking coffee and thinking about the woman on the billboard.

Miss Malibu Waterbeds had to be Bobby's driver.

The problem was, Bad Company's brain wasn't working exactly right.

His brain got like this every once in a while.

More, recently.

He remembered drinking gin and beer last night. He still felt slightly like shit.

Big Bobby's driver was the woman on the billboard.

Malibu Fucking Waterbeds.

Wet and wild when you want.

Where was that?

Speedway, like everything else.

So what. The ad could have been made in Chicago.

Except it was the same woman. The woman

behind the wheel of the Chevette.

With the pearls.

It was starting to get hot again. Even here in air conditioned Mother Hubbard's.

It was October, what the hell was this? Everything was supposed to be nice and cool here in Tucson. Now it was heating up again. Bad Company felt sweat under his denims. His hangover was sticking around longer than usual.

Gin and beer. He needed to knock that shit off.

He had lived in Arizona all his life but that didn't mean he liked the heat.

Bad Company didn't like hot weather at all and he didn't like being outside in the heat.

It was a good thing Bad Company was big.

Being a bouncer was inside work.

He had a three word resume.

Big, imposing, scary.

He was glad he had come to Tucson instead of Phoenix .

The Crazy Horse was okay.

College kids and goat ropers.

Wet T-shirt contests.

What the hell more do you want?

The waitress stood next to Bad Company. He heard her voice.

He had been dozing. He felt better than when he had come in.

"I'll take the check," he said.

He dropped the cigarette in the ashtray.

Put a ten-spot on the table.

BEWITCHED

Malibu Waterbeds was snazzier than Bad Company expected.

The waterbeds were displayed on the floor just like they were waiting for you to lie on them, each bed displaying a cardboard sign telling you not to wear your shoes.

Like Goldilocks and the Three Bears.

This one's just right.

Bad Company looked at his engineer boots. Nobody was going to make Bad Company take his boots off.

Not unless he said so.

No sign of the blonde woman who advertised the beds on television.

The same woman who wore the bikini on the billboards.

A salesman with a tag saying his name was Tex came up to Bad Company.

He didn't look like anybody named Tex.

The salesman was in the low five foot category.

Cop moustache. Short center-part hair. Protruding teeth. Young. His Malibu Waterbed golf shirt made him look even younger.

He was all business.

A young Dale Carnegie, ready to make a sale.

"Can I help you?" Tex said.

"I don't want to talk to you," Bad Company said. "I want to talk to *her*."

Bad Company pointed at a brunette on the other side of the room. The woman was talking and laughing with another customer. She hadn't noticed him yet. Not the woman on the television ads, but a lot like her. Like Samantha when she put on her wig in *Bewitched* to play Serena.

Wet and wild when you want.

Tex looked at Bad Company like he was used to this.

"Lydia's our manager. Looks like she's tied up right now," Tex said. "Maybe I can help you. Show you around. Have you been in before?"

Bad Company looked at Tex.

Tex gave a weak grin.

"What's your name?" Tex said. "I can tell her you're here."

"They call me Bad Company. She's expecting me."

Tex looked at him.

Put the clipboard to his side. Nodded.

"Okay," he said. "Make yourself comfortable. Look around. Looks like she'll be free pretty soon."

"No man," Bad Company said. "I can't wait. I'll catch her another time. Don't say nothing."

Bad Company looked at the woman again.

It had to be her.

A woman could do a lot with a wig. He'd seen it before. Who hadn't? You watch television, you're going to see that gimmick. Writers can't come up with something new, they put the actress in a different wig and give her a different personality.

Bewitched, they'd done it.

Patty Duke Show, they did it. Identical cousins, whatever *they* were.

Maybe this woman had a split personality like the *Three Faces of Eve*.

That was real.

Bad Company even read about it in Psychology Today. He forgot what they called it, but it was real. You got two personalities in your head, and half the time they don't even know the other one is there. He was pretty sure he'd seen it in the bar, too. Women came in wearing blonde wigs like they were *I Dream of Jeannie*. Lots of fun.

Tex looked at Bad Company who was walking toward the door.

"Hold on."

Bad Company heard the woman's voice coming from across the showroom.

"She's got ears on her, doesn't she?" Tex said. "She don't like seeing anybody go out the door."

She stood in front of him.

Same height, same size, same face.

Everything but the hair the same. But she wasn't the same woman. This wasn't the driver.

She didn't have the sexy look like the woman had.

"Can we show anything to you?"

She looked at him.

Bad Company started to say something, then stopped. It wasn't the same woman so what was he doing here?

"You ever put a waterbed in a van?"

He knew it sounded stupid as soon as he said it.

"Some people do," she said. "Tex can help you. Don't forget to sign up for our drawing."

She walked away.

Tex held a clipboard.

"It's a drawing. You could win a waterbed." He pushed the clipboard into Bad Company's hands. "I've seen some pictures of beds in vans. It's kinda a specialty thing."

Bad Company wrote his real name on one of the tickets on the clipboard.

What the hell, he could win. He put the address and phone number of the Crazy Horse.

"That's all right, Tex. No sweat. I gotta go, I'll let you know if I want to try that."

"You bet, sir." Tex smiled. He held the door for Bad Company and handed him a card.

The name on the card was Lydia Partridge.

"That's her card," Tex said. He grinned again. "I'm new here, but if you call, ask for Tex."

* * *

Bad Company was good at waiting.

There was a pay phone at the end of the block

from the waterbed company, next to a payday loan place. He gave it a few minutes.

Too quick, and she might not go for it.

Bad Company dropped a quarter in the slot, looked at the card, pushed in the numbers.

Asked for Lydia.

He said what he had to say.

"Your sister," he said. "Your sister needs you pretty bad. You better get over here quick. I'm at her place. There's a problem with her."

Lydia didn't answer him at once.

There was a pause on the phone.

Bad Company smiled, picturing her.

Not so confident now, was she?

"Who is this?" she said.

He didn't bother answering.

He didn't need to. They were sisters.

He hung up.

Bad Company was prepared to wait as long as it took. He had a couple slices of OD pizza from Last Chance in the back of the van.

KWFM.

All the Young Dudes.

He didn't have to wait long.

Lydia was out in a few minutes, smoothing the front of her black skirt, walking to her car in the high heels.

Bad Company watched her go to her car.

She was as sexy as her sister.

She just showed it differently.

BONUS JACK

Grace's apartment was all orange and white shag and Calvin had been cooped up there since the heist.

He had worked his way around every inch of the apartment's interior with a burglar's instinct.

He needed a trip outside.

The apartment was like a prison.

Almost.

He wasn't locked in.

He could come and go as he pleased. But staying in the apartment was the smart move.

He should have felt good.

The bank job was a success.

They were just laying low.

He had to get out of the apartment before going crazy.

Calvin lay bare-chested on the orange sectional, blowing smoke rings toward the ceiling.

Grace had provided him with cigarettes, beer, and a Thai stick.

Orange and white.

Orange and white.

Orange and white.

Like a one bedroom creamsicle.

Orange was Grace's power color, whatever that meant.

He had to get out, go somewhere.

Anywhere.

The Jack in the Box closest to Grace's apartment had the same color scheme as Grace's apartment, but more of a burnt orange.

"Jack in the Box may I take your order?"

The kid behind the counter must have been seventeen.

His nametag read Charles.

Charles was skinny, red-haired, and had big knuckles. Charles looked like he spent a lot of time cracking them.

"I'll go with the beef burrito, Bonus Jack, three tacos, and a vanilla shake," Calvin said.

Jack in the Box was cheap.

Change came back from Calvin's ten.

Calvin looked around the brightly lit restaurant.

He liked Jack in the Box. It wasn't fussy.

Despite the name, the place wasn't just for children. Calvin had nothing against children, but found fast-food playgrounds nauseating.

"Here you go, sir. Anything else?"

Charles looked at Calvin.

Calvin was thinking about how easy the bank job had been. Charles would be amazed if he knew he was serving a successful bank robber.

There wouldn't be anything like the amount of cash at a Jack in the Box as you'd find at a bank, but then again, he and Grace could do a job like a Jack in the Box by themselves.

It was something to consider.

Calvin needed to remember to discuss it with Grace.

Knocking over a couple places like this might be a good sendoff for their Mexican cruise.

It felt good being out of the apartment, but Calvin decided to take the Bonus Jack and the shake back.

He sat on the sectional again, the Jack in the Box bag in front of him.

Watching television.

Love Boat.

The knock on the front door of the apartment startled Calvin.

He would ignore it.

Jo Anne Worley and Charles Nelson Reilly were doing some shit in their cabin.

Calvin hated Charles Nelson Reilly.

Why did they even put him on these shows? Did *anybody* like seeing Charles Nelson Reilly?

No, they didn't.

Calvin grabbed the remote and turned on Days of Our Lives.

The woman on the show looked upset.

Something was going on with her and the man she was talking to.

Calvin was about to change the station again when the waterbed commercial came on.

There she was.

Grace.

Wet and wild.

She really was something.

Calvin heard another knock. He couldn't ignore it.

This time it was loud.

CASA BONITA

Lydia, the waterbed manager, stood outside her sister's apartment. Bad Company watched her. Tailing her Datsun hadn't been difficult. Lydia had been focused on getting to her sister's house.

Miss Waterbed Store Manager didn't even look in her rear-view.

She didn't see the Econoline with Bad Company behind the wheel.

She was an impatient driver. She crept up behind cars stopped in front of her at stoplights, rocking those high heels back and forth on the accelerator.

Signaling her turns too far in advance.

She was easy to follow.

Bad Company himself never used a turn signal.

He felt they showed a lack of confidence so he just didn't use them.

Lydia was different from her sister, but man, they looked alike.

She pulled in at the Casa Bonita apartments, and Bad Company kept going, pulling his van into the service alley just past the complex. There was space in front of the dumpsters and Bad Company got out and walked toward the apartments.

Next to the pool a couple of women were sunning. Bad Company looked them over. One of the women in a bikini and the other in a striped one-piece. Neither of the women was the driver.

Lydia was walking up the stairs. She stood in front of one of the front doors and knocked. This was as much information as Bad Company needed. He could have left then, but he waited.

Lydia kept knocking.

Bad Company saw the door open.

The man standing at the door was Bud.

Whatever his real name was.

The one with the grease gun.

He and Lydia were talking a while.

Lydia turned away from the door. She stood on the upper walkway.

Except for her dark hair, Lydia looked just like the driver.

DAYTIME TELEVISION

Calvin went back to the sectional.

Maybe it was time to roll another doob.

Grace's dope wasn't half bad, although not as good as Grace thought.

The woman at the door was a surprise.

Grace's sister.

She wouldn't come in. Calvin asked her a couple of times. She looked at Calvin like he was a serial killer.

Funny when you thought about it. Calvin had been on Lydia's bed with Grace just days ago and now Lydia comes up to the door all high and mighty.

She didn't even ask who he was. Just kept saying something about a phone call.

Calvin hadn't called her. How would he know who had?

After he convinced Lydia Grace wasn't here, she left. Calvin watched her from behind the curtain in the apartment.

Lydia was nice looking, just like Grace, but she was high-strung.

The thing about a phone call. What was that all about?

Calvin pulled the ice cube tray out from beneath the couch and scraped the remnants of the Thai stick together.

Rolled the joint and licked it.

He wasn't going to worry about anything.

It was probably nothing.

Grace had taken charge of the bank money, counting it, re-banding it, putting it in a new overnight bag she bought at Jewelcor. She brought two bags back to the apartment, but once she started stacking the money, it was clear only one was needed.

Calvin watched her. She could have been playing monopoly, except these were real bills.

"It looks better than that duffel bag, right?" Grace said.

"Sure does," Calvin said.

She knew how to do things.

Calvin remembered Big Bobby holding the duffel bag next to his shitty apartment. Grace was lucky Calvin had come along.

Big Bobby had been second rate.

"Grace," he said, "do you feel like some things were just meant to be?"

"I'm trusting you, Bud," she said. "I'm working on something else, so I'm going to have to trust you here, right?"

Calvin laughed.

"Don't worry a minute about anything, Grace," he said, "you got my word."

Calvin wasn't just talking. He had no intention to double-cross Grace. He liked being with her and he was looking forward to the cruise. Calvin had never been on a cruise. He had watched *Love Boat* enough, but he was sure the real thing was better.

"I have a special place for this, Calvin." She picked up the Jewelcor bag. She had bundled the money tightly and it all fit. It was the size bag you could put above your seat on a Greyhound bus.

Grace took him into the kitchen.

She took the cleaning supplies out from beneath the sink. Calvin was surprised how many products she had under there. She hadn't used them very much. She lifted the base of the cupboard, revealing a false bottom.

Just big enough for the Jewelcor case.

Calvin looked at the hiding place.

It was okay. Not great, but okay.

If he'd broken in here he would have found the spot, but then, Calvin was a pro and this kind of thing was his bread and butter.

"You don't have to worry, about anything, Grace," he said. "I'm here."

"This guy I'm talking to, he's interested in some artwork. A painting up in the foothills. Think you might be interested?"

"Depends," Calvin said. "I was thinking you and I would just go to Mexico."

"We can, Bud," she said. "This would just be for fun money."

* * *

Calvin Gamble had been surprised how little attention the killings up in Catalina had gotten. He figured that kind of body count should have made a bigger splash in the papers, but it hadn't.

Just business as usual in the drug underworld of Tucson. The police hadn't made any connection between Catalina and the bank job in Casas Adobes.

Calvin and Grace had burned the Chevette.

They doused the car inside and out with gasoline, lighted it, then drove back to Grace's crib in Calvin's Country Squire.

Calvin hadn't seen much of Grace since then, but this was the way she wanted it.

She didn't mind him staying in her place. She liked it.

It made sense for the two of them to lay low a little.

They would keep out of sight for a while, then book a Mexican cruise under assumed names.

Calvin spent some time thinking of a new name for himself.

He kept coming back to the name Pablo, but he realized Pablo was a Mexican name. The name might imply he spoke Spanish and could lead to complications when it turned out he could not.

Better to stick with the name Bud.

Grace was used to calling him Bud and Calvin liked the way the name sounded when she said it.

The apartment was okay.

Except Grace was a slob.

There were dishes everywhere in and out of the kitchen.

Calvin was stuck with daytime television and what was left of the Thai stick.

In the courtyard of the apartment there was a pool, but Calvin knew it would be foolish to be seen outside. He stayed inside while Grace was away from the apartment. A couple of flight attendants had an apartment in the complex and Calvin watched them in their blue uniforms and later, when they were splashing around in the pool.

Calvin had been thinking about the flight attendants while Grace gave him the new plan.

"It's safe," she said. "We can't be indiscriminate, Bud. We just can't do that."

Calvin nodded.

You had to remember to call them flight attendants now.

No more stewardesses.

Coffee, tea, or me, Bud?

"Bud, are you listening to me?"

He told her of course he was listening to her.

Calvin was committed to sticking with Grace, but she wasn't making things easy.

Grace was a hell of a woman, but Calvin wasn't really used to working with anyone.

Plus, she'd taken off and left him here.

It was getting on his nerves, even after Jack in the Box.

For the second time in an hour, somebody was knocking on the door.

What the hell was this?

Had Lydia decided to come back?

ANSWERING
MACHINE

Lydia Partridge stood on the tile floor in her kitchen holding Trinity's card. She had come home after going to her sister's apartment.

Trinity's recorded voice was the way she remembered. Calm, reassuring.

She left a message.

Lydia knew she sounded like she was out of breath. It didn't matter. She couldn't explain everything in a message.

She asked him to call her.

Lydia gave him her phone number, told him her address. She closed her eyes.

She thought about the man at Grace's apartment.

He didn't look right.

He wasn't right.

She was thinking about the phone call she'd gotten at work. The guy on the phone saying Grace needed her.

Nothing made sense.

She needed Trinity.

KNOCKING

Bad Company had the gun in his right hand.

Knocking on the front door of the apartment.

The women sunning at the pool weren't looking at him. They hadn't seen him.

Bud was in there.

Bad Company knocked again. He could stay here all day, but he didn't think he would.

He'd give Bud another minute before knocking the door down.

He held the .22 at his side. He'd fitted it with a homemade silencer.   No need to disturb the sunbathers.

Unless the asshole jumped out the back window, he was still in the apartment.

The woman wasn't there.

Just the asshole.

Maybe the money.

Hopefully the money.

VITRUVIAN MAN

Frank Trinity gripped the handle of the axe in the palm of his right hand, letting the two and a half pound blade hang down beside his knee. He let his shoulders roll back, squaring them to a target he had placed fifteen feet in front of him.

Controlling his breathing, he rolled his shoulders forwards and backwards. Feeling his inhalation and exhalation, making his mind a blank. Picturing the axe buried in the solar plexus of Vitruvian Man.

It was a beautiful morning in Trinity's Presidio neighborhood.

As beautiful a day as Tucson could ever offer.

The lime tree was bearing fruit. It reminded Trinity of the hotel where he and Valerie had stayed in the south of France.

A pension in Roussillon.

The weather was cool. Normal for October.

Trinity caught himself.

Tried to empty his mind of all thoughts the way Mr. Yee had taught him.

Before any throw, the mind needed to be calm and free from chatter.

No matter what you were throwing.

A solitary cicada was making a racket in the mesquite on Trinity's right side.

Interrupting him just at the wrong moment.

✤ ✤ ✤

Trinity had created a pine target backed by stacked bales of hay. The target worked, but he needed more hay. He had bought the wood at Grant Road Lumber and the bales of hay at the OK Feed Lot on Oracle, hauling it all back to the Presidio in the Bronco, the lumber precariously held on top with bungee cords and luck.

The target stood in the back yard.

Vitruvian Man.

The likeness wasn't bad at all.

Trinity's neighbor Leonard Blue had watched from across the street while Trinity took the lumber and the hay out of the Bronco.

Leonard, with a joint hanging from his mouth had been typing. He had been busy the last couple of months rewriting his self-described masterpiece.

Sidewalk Dharma.

Leonard made a career of staying out of the way of his wife Karma Blue.

Making himself scarce when Karma Blue started her frequent tirades.

Sometimes, Leonard stayed on the scaffolding in front of his house for hours at a time.

"Hey Trinity," Leonard said. "You building an ark?"

Trinity looked at Leonard.

A joke, but Leonard looked curious.

"Sure, Leonard," Trinity said. "That's what I'm doing. Monsoons are going to be extra long this year. You and Karma Blue may want to build one."

Trinity pointed at the stack of wood.

"This is just a start."

"The hay's for what, the livestock?" Leonard Blue said. "You're gonna need more hay."

"It's on the list, Leonard," Trinity said.

Leonard stretched out on the scaffolding.

"You know what, Trinity? You need something to keep you busy, man. You ever thought about taking up meditation?"

"I meditate," Trinity said. "I'm meditating right now."

Leonard Blue shook his head.

"That's what I mean, Trinity. You're uptight. Listen. One of these days you're going to get sick of this rush-rush world you've created for yourself. And then what's left, man? What's left after that?"

∗ ∗ ∗

Trinity concentrated.

Trying to forget about his earlier conversation with Leonard.

Forgetting about meditation.

Forgetting he needed more hay.

Forgetting how he would have to collect both male and female of every species to populate a proper ark.

Putting everything out of his mind, exactly the way Mr. Yee taught him years ago at Camp Long.

How was Mr. Yee getting along? He was the one person he really missed from his year in Korea.

Mr. Yee was one in a million.

An investigator's investigator, Trinity had learned a lot from him.

So, Trinity wondered how Mr. Yee was doing now.

Trinity put the question out of his mind.

Dismissed the question as firmly as Mr. Yee himself would have directed.

Trinity was beginning to realize that as a meditative exercise, throwing the axe might be a flop.

He hadn't been able to focus at all.

Maybe Leonard Blue was right.

Everything came into Trinity's mind. None of it left.

Most of his thoughts were unimportant.

Just clutter, turning and spinning.

Mr. Yee would not approve.

Trinity pulled his arm up to appraise the target.

Time spent after the initial glance took away concentration.

More wisdom from Mr. Yee.

Trinity brought the axe slowly upward.

Held it aloft.

Yee could throw an ordinary pocket knife across a room and into the center of the ace of spades. Just a regular folding knife, the kind you could get for seven or eight bucks at the PX.

Mr. Yee could throw anything with accuracy.

A quick glance upward and Trinity saw the tip of the axe blade.

One second.

Two seconds.

Trinity held the axe as if he were frozen.

Then he dropped his arm.

He wasn't ready.

Vitruvian Man was spared.

* * *

The telephone was ringing.

Trinity thought about letting it go directly to the message he'd recorded.

One ring. Two rings.

Trinity carefully put the axe down on the drop-leaf table next to his throwing knife.

The knife was backup.

The interruption was irritating.

He stepped inside to answer the phone.

Trinity wasn't quick enough. By the time he reached the phone the ringing had stopped. The machine was recording a message.

Fine.

He went back into the kitchen, poured a cup of

coffee from the percolator, pushed the button on top of the flashing answering machine.

He was making too much of the whole axe business.

No need going all *Kung Fu* about it. Mr. Yee wouldn't approve of that, either.

The woman's voice made him stand still.

Trinity was paying attention. He felt a chill.

"Frank Trinity?" she said. "Do you remember me? We met a couple of nights ago at El Charro?

The woman with the sister.

Trinity recognized her voice. Lower now. Measured. Less of a sales pitch in her voice.

"Can you call me?" she said.

She gave him two numbers.

One for the store, one for home.

Trinity looked around for a pen. Leaned over the counter and copied the numbers.

"I need your help, Trinity," she said. "I really need your help."

Trinity put the pen down.

Picked up the cup of coffee.

He walked back behind the house and stared at the target.

Vitruvian Man.

Legs and arms spread.

Trinity picked up the axe. Held it over his head.

He couldn't empty his mind, but he didn't care.

He liked her. They had only spoken briefly at the restaurant, but Trinity liked Lydia.

He liked the way she looked and he liked her

spirit.

He was glad she had called.

He felt the weight of the axe.

Throwing an axe was like riding a bicycle if you've never ridden a bicycle before.

Except Trinity had done this.

He'd learned the skill from the best teacher he'd ever known.

Mr. Yee.

Knives, axes, even a mess hall fork, if there was nothing else. Mr. Yee could throw anything.

Mr. Yee would have made a hell of a pitcher, but he'd grown up after the war and he didn't have time to play games. He'd gone to work on Camp Long and been there ever since.

Mr. Yee taught Trinity how to throw.

Visualize the thrown object reaching and penetrating the intended target.

Long, dark, cold winter nights, Trinity had practiced.

Picking up the knife without touching it.

Slowing the pace of the projectile in your mind and then launching it with the strength of ten men.

"Ten lions," Mr. Yee had said. "Ten lions lie deep in your body. Find them and let them do the work."

Trinity laughed, but Mr. Yee had not been joking.

❊ ❊ ❊

He had known he would hear from Lydia

Partridge.

Trinity's axe reached the target.

The blade buried deep in the heart of Vitruvian Man.

Her sister was her problem.

The one in the waterbed ad.

Grace Partridge.

Trinity remembered her name.

He walked away from the target, then stopped.

Trinity whirled quickly on the heel of his boot and threw the knife.

A split-second jugular hit.

The knife quivered in the target, coming to rest in the neck of *Vitruvian Man*.

LOVE BOAT

Calvin placed the joint in the orange ashtray in front of the sectional.

Knocking, again.

Fuck this.

Calvin didn't feel like getting up again.

The ashtray was already full, but Calvin was not going to empty it.

He picked up the remote control from the coffee table and turned off the television.

Whoever was knocking on the door wasn't going to stop.

A big heavy knock like a cop might use, but Calvin knew it wasn't cops.

Calvin looked at the door again.

Picked up the joint again.

It was funny neither Grace nor Lydia slept on a waterbed.

It seemed like you should stand behind your product, anyway.

You sell waterbeds, you should sleep on one.

More knocking.

If he ignored the knocking maybe it would stop.

Looked at the paper again.

The bank robbery and the killings in Catalina were just two separate incidents.

Nothing tied the two together.

He had Big Bobby to thank for that. At least Big Bobby was good about planning the job out.

Calvin shook his head.

He loved thinking about Bobby's reaction to the grease gun.

Bobby had a problem with the gun?

Bobby had had no idea what his *real* problem was.

Big Bobby's problem was Grace, and he hadn't lived long enough to figure that out.

Calvin was glad Grace was on his side.

Calvin got up.

Love Boat was still on with a different episode.

This one was Judy Carne and Robert Goulet.

He scratched his chest, walked to the door.

Whoever was out there was persistent.

Before he opened the door, he looked out the window.

Calvin saw the big man holding the gun down, like he wasn't supposed to see it.

Calvin recognized him.

Bad Company had a gun.

BATHROOM WINDOW

You go into burglary, you need to know how to get out the back. Calvin was a pro.

Bad Company.

It would have been better if it had been police.

He had to go out a different way.

The knocking stopped.

Calvin knew better than to think Bad Company had left.

Calvin headed for the bathroom window.

Even a drop from there would be his best chance of escape.

He had to get back to the kitchen.

He threw the cleaning products on the floor and grabbed the Jewelcor bag.

He heard the first kick on the door.

Calvin could tell the difference between Bad Company knocking on the door and starting to kick it down.

He ran to the bathroom. Stood on the edge of the bathtub and bashed at the screen.

The thing wasn't opening like it should.

He heard the front door splinter.

The screen popped out, and Calvin tossed it on the tiles outside the tub.

Bad Company was in the apartment.

Calvin looked at the window. Too big for him to get out with the bag. He looked back at the bathroom door, sure he would see Bad Company.

Bad Company wasn't going to negotiate.

Calvin didn't even look in the alley before throwing the bag out the window.

The opening was much smaller than he thought.

He hung to the window for a second before letting go.

AIRPORT

Grace Partridge was at the airport.

She had bought her ticket using a different name that she would be using for a while.

She held her bag. It was all she carried, but she didn't need anything else. She hadn't known what else to do.

Bud scared her.

He'd killed Bobby and the others without hesitation. What would keep Bud from killing her?

How had this started?

A few drinks at the Western Way and listening to Big Bobby's plan.

Then she'd changed things.

She'd gotten greedy. Brought in Bud.

Bud was probably looking for her now. Maybe he would team up with Bad Company.

Her flight was being announced. She started for the gate.

With her new name, he wouldn't find her.

But he could find Lydia.

Grace looked at the row of pay telephones. She needed to call Lydia at least.

Call her and warn her.

CLOSE-UP MAGIC

Calvin opened the bag.

The guns were in the Country Squire.

He had a room at Mi Casita Motel.

He shook the crumpled pieces of newsprint on the bathroom floor.

It felt like weeks since he'd bought the guns.

He still had money, but it was running low.

The Arizona Daily Star.

Each piece like confetti. He hadn't thought about the difference in weight.

She'd fooled him. Done a little close-up magic on Calvin. A few bills on top, the rest was newsprint.

She was something else, man.

Calling him Bud.

He had gone back to the apartment later. After Bad Company left.

Calvin didn't have the key, but so what? He'd gone in, anyway. No sign of Grace.

He could wait here as long as he wanted, she wouldn't be coming back.

Calvin looked down at the pieces of newspaper. He wasn't able to bring himself to throw it away.

"Guess she's got all of it," he said. He kicked the

paper away with the toe of his boot and took the remote control from the side of the bed.

Turned on the color television.

There she was.

Standing, facing the camera.

Her voice low and sensual.

"We're wet and wild... When you want."

ECONOLINE

The Crazy Horse was deserted except for one daytime drinker at the end of the bar and the bartender. A tarp was thrown over the mechanical bull.

Calvin had never been here this early.

A poster on the wall advertised a wet T-shirt contest held a week ago.

Calvin had missed watching the contest. He hadn't even seen the poster before today.

This place was different during daylight hours.

Calvin got a Coors and pointed at the poster.

"I missed that," he said. "You coulda put the poster up earlier or something."

"Life's tough," the bartender said.

"Where's the guy here at night?" Calvin said. "Bad Company."

The bartender shrugged.

"Out back," he said. "Probably in his van."

"Guy's name is Bad Company?" the daytime drinker said. "That's a hell of a name, isn't it?

"His name's Raymond," the bartender said.

He held his index finger to his lips.

"That's kinda secret."

Calvin slid off the barstool.

Took the beer with him and went back to the Country Squire.

With Bad Company still on the scene, Calvin would never be safe.

He would find the money.

Grace wasn't going to be able to hide forever. But he wasn't going to look over his shoulder for the rest of his life. Not for a lousy forty grand.

Calvin got out of his car.

The back of the bar was in an alley. A couple of dumpsters and some weeds.

The Econoline was there. Bad Company had a folding chair outside the van.

He looked up when he saw Calvin.

Bad Company didn't even look surprised when Calvin took out the Semmerling

PAY PHONE

There was only one L. Partridge in the phone book.

She answered on the second ring.

"Your sister's gone," Calvin said. "She took something of mine. Mind if I come get it?"

Calvin looked at the street from the phone booth.

Going to Lydia's place had started all this.

"Who is this?" Lydia said.

Calvin hung up the phone and laughed.

PRESIDIO

"They think I know where she is." Lydia said.

"Do you?" Trinity said.

He was sitting on a wooden chair in her row house. She was drinking red wine and had made coffee for Trinity.

She looked at him.

"Do I what?"

"Do you know where she is?" Trinity said.

Lydia shook her head no. She didn't know. The story was too crazy. Her sister disappeared and left Lydia with an impossible story.

A frantic call.

Incomplete and incomprehensible.

"She said I should watch out for these two. I know what they look like. I've seen both of them."

Lydia described Calvin and Bad Company.

"Which one do you think called?"

"I think it was the one who was at her place. He had the same voice."

She really wasn't sure.

Grace hadn't told Lydia where she was.

She didn't tell Lydia anything except to watch out for the two men.

Grace had been involved with something terrible and she had something the men wanted.

"She kept saying how sorry she was," Lydia said. "She kept saying it, like if she said it enough times she would mean it."

The room was dark. A small framed saint stared at Trinity.

"They're going to kill her when they find her," she said. "Isn't that right?"

Trinity nodded. People kill for very small reasons. Sometimes they kill for no reason at all.

"Why did she tell you all this?"

Lydia looked at him.

She had the same expression as the other night. This time, Trinity understood why.

"She tells me everything," Lydia said. "We've never had secrets from each other."

She stopped. Looked at her hands.

"Except now, I guess."

"I see."

Trinity looked around the room.

Dark adobe walls lined with saints.

"Can you help me?"

Trinity stood up. Touched the cool stucco of the nearest wall.

Put his hat on. Walked to the window.

"I can help."

"Whatever you need," she said, "I can pay whatever you need."

Trinity turned and looked at Lydia.

"How about we figure that part out later?"

DOUBLE VISION

Somewhere past nine o'clock, Calvin figured it out. He was drinking an umbrella drink on Miracle Mile near Mi Casita. It was a place with nets and cork.

He wasn't going to get drunk tonight. He wanted a good start in the morning.

He would to take the Country Squire and get out on the open road.

Leave Tucson.

Now he'd figured it out, it was pretty obvious.

It wasn't the first time he'd thought of it, but he'd pushed it out of his mind.

The two women were nearly identical.

The sisters.

The one sister worked at the waterbed store.

The other was an actress.

"Nope," Calvin said.

The waitress looked at him.

"No more?" she said.

"Nope," Calvin said, "I was talking to myself. Come back in a second. I might just want another."

He would only have one more tonight.

He needed to get to work.

He knew where the money was, and she wasn't going to get away with it.

* * *

The shower at Mi Casita didn't have excellent pressure, but the water was hot.

Calvin already felt half-sober.

He rubbed the pink bar of soap on his chest.

It had been interesting working with Grace, but Calvin was glad he was working alone again.

SHADOWS

Calvin looked around with the flashlight. The same pictures of saints hanging on the walls. Just as weird tonight.

He'd earned forty grand, for a while.

He stood in front of the front door.

Thought about knocking. Decided against it.

Picked the lock.

Easy as pie.

The Semmerling was in his pocket.

A powerful weapon for something so small.

This place was quiet.

In a way, he hoped she *was* home.

The actress.

She pulled a con on him, hadn't she? She got him to do her dirty work, and all along she planned to keep the money.

Pretending she had a sister.

They were the same person.

Calvin knew if he looked around the place, he would find a wig.

And he would get his forty thousand.

He would have shared with her.

But not now.

The place was black. Calvin took out his flashlight and started to look around.

Maybe she put a little hiding place under the sink here, too.

He was pointing the flashlight from side to side when the lights went on and he saw her.

Looking at him from the bedroom where he'd seen her first.

There was no doubt in his mind they were the same woman.

He didn't have time to reach for the Semmerling.

He heard the man's voice behind him and felt the cold barrel of a gun next to his head.

"Hands up," the man said.

The man had come in behind him.

He'd been standing in the shadows almost as if he'd been waiting for Calvin.

Calvin slowly put up his hands and turned slightly.

The gun was pointed directly at Calvin's head.

CORNER MARKET

Trinity bought a morning paper. He was sitting next to the front window at the Corner Market. Two young women at the table next to him were chatting behind glasses of iced tea. One of them, a blonde, wore a pink sorority sweatshirt. Recognizing the Greek letters, Trinity looked at her more carefully. He recognized her.

She didn't see Trinity.

The young woman looked like a happy, well-adjusted member of the university community.

Last night, Trinity had sat in his Bronco outside Lydia's house and waited.

Not too long, though.

The man had come earlier than Trinity thought he would. Lydia had given a good description. Now Calvin Gamble was at the police station downtown.

Trinity knew there would be a lot more to the story. Already, he knew something about what had happened.

A man named Raymond "Bad Company" Moore had been shot earlier outside a bar and was in critical condition. There was a connection between the shooting and three recent deaths. One in the foothills, two in Catalina. They would figure it out downtown.

Calvin Gamble wasn't Trinity's business.

Trinity had his own story.

He lived in the same neighborhood as Lydia and had seen something while he was passing by. Being an observant neighbor he had investigated what had turned out to be an intruder.

Neighbors should look out for one another, shouldn't they?

Grace Partridge could be anywhere by now.

He would approach the matter delicately with Lydia. She might not see her sister again for a long time. Possibly she would never see her again.

It was a shame. Grace had sold her life cheaply. Trinity tried to look at it differently, but could see Grace's situation no other way.

Trinity looked at the newspaper.

The front page picture showed an ambulance behind the Crazy Horse.

Shooting at Popular Night Spot.

Trinity put the paper down. He would read the article later.

McIndoe Falls, Vermont
11/16/2020

BOOKS BY THIS AUTHOR

Trinity Works Alone

Trinity Thinks Twice

Trinity And The Short-Timer

Trinity Springs Forward

Ferguson's Trip

Dim Lights Thick Smoke

Lefty And The Killers

A note to the reader:

Thank you for reading this book.

If you enjoyed *Trinity and the Heisters*, please consider writing a short review on Amazon and telling your friends. As Walter Tevis, writer of *The Hustler* and *The Queen's Gambit* wrote: "word of mouth is an author's best friend and much appreciated."

Trevor Holliday

Printed in Great Britain
by Amazon

27201668R00096